The RADIUS

Initiative

J. CHAD BARRETT

ISBN: 061559364X

ISBN-13: 9780615593647

To order more copies of The RADIUS Initiative visit

www.InspiringEvangelism.com.

To the Church

CHAPTER ONE

Friday, August 5, 2005. Occobamba, Apurimac, Peru, South America

The air was thin, and the sun was out in the high altitude of the Andes Mountains of Peru. For flatlanders, this made breathing quite difficult and sun screen vital. It was truly amazing to see sixty-foot trees grow at this altitude, and the lush, greenery of the landscape made picture-perfect postcards.

The small village of Occobamba sat nestled at 11,000 feet among these tall trees and a wide variety of vegetation. Mud houses adorned the hills, and colorful gardens sketched the slopes all around the village. A dark, leathery-skinned woman drove cattle along the dirt road leading up to the village. She carried her baby on her back with a beautifully colored blanket—red, blue, purple, and gold.

Near the highest point of the village sat an old, wooden church house. It appeared to have been painted a hundred years ago, and there was a three-foot mud wall that made a large yard on the side of the building. Inside the dirt yard and underneath an overhang of the building sat three women around a fire. They were skinning guinea pigs and boiling potatoes for supper.

Two older-modeled Toyota minivans were parked outside. Inside the church house were several worn out, wooden benches and a podium up front. Two dim light fixtures hung from wires stretched across the bare ceiling. Fifteen children huddled on a dirt floor. The church house also served as an orphanage, and missionaries from the United Adoption Agency in the United States were praying over the children.

All the children had their eyes closed except for Kristina. With her hands folded, she peeked around to see if anyone else had their eyes open. Her best friend, Isabella, was kneeling right beside her. She noticed Kristina looking around, nudged her, and said, "Cierra los ojos!" Kristina immediately closed her eyes.

The missionaries took turns praying in Spanish for the orphaned children who were about to be sent to New Orleans for six weeks. Each child had high hopes for being adopted. They were excited to go, and the missionaries were eager to provide the best care possible.

As the missionaries finished praying, the wind began to pick up and a strange energy flowed gently through the room. The lights flickered a few times, and everyone looked around with wonder and slight concern.

The front door of the old adobe house slowly creaked opened, and an elderly woman stepped inside and approached the huddle. Every eye followed her as she entered the room. She wore a typical Peruvian, multicolored blanket over her head and around her shoulders. She had no shoes, and her feet were like dark, worn leather. But her eyes sparkled like stars on the darkest of nights.

She approached the huddle as if summoned. She stretched out her hands, laying one on a missionary and the other on a child. Then she prayed in her native Quechuan language. As she prayed, a translator leaned in close to another missionary.

"She is praying for the protection of the children," the translator whispered. "She said she has heard of predators stealing orphans, but she is thankful for the United Adoption Agency and their hard work to keep these children safe. She prays for the good health of the children. And she especially prays for them to be free of all harm."

"Who is she?" asked the missionary.

"I don't know. I've never seen her before."

When the old woman finished her prayer, she kissed each child on the forehead and walked out of the front door.

Minutes later, the children were loaded into the minivans with what little luggage they owned. Many from the village gathered to say good-bye. With tears in their eyes the orphanage workers hugged and kissed the children. They were all hoping this short journey to the States would turn into a permanent adoption by a loving, Christian family. The vans took their leave down the long, winding, and dangerous mountain roads of the Andes, as everyone else stood behind and waved.

As the vans left with the children, the missionary looked around for the elderly Quechuan woman, but she was nowhere to be seen.

Three Weeks Later— Nizhny, Novgorod Oblast, Russia

A tall man with a gray beard and black-rimmed eye glasses picked up the ringing telephone from his desk.

"Da. Sokolov."

"I hear you are not pleased with your findings," said a man with a strong, middle-eastern accent.

"I will have what you need quite soon. I need more time and more test subjects."

"I have provided you village in Sweden, and I pay you well. What more do you want? And where will you acquire next victims?" asked the man. "I was understanding this condition is very rare."

"It is rare, Amir, but I have found one more cluster. I have to go now. I will be in touch soon." Dr. Sokolov hung up his phone. "Afon," he said.

"Yes, Father," answered Afon.

"Our plane leaves in 1 hour. Go ready our driver. I will be with you momentarily."

Friday, August 26, 2005. New Orleans, Louisiana

Naomi answered her cell. A male voice was heard on the other end, "Hey, Sis. What are you planning to do?"

"Hey, I don't know. They came by and we talked, but I don't feel good about this. Please tell me you've decided to evacuate. This is really troubling me."

"Naomi, we'll be fine. I can handle it. Now tell me why you don't feel good about contacting the FBI."

"Well—they kept asking weird questions. Wanted to know who my husband was. And they wanted a list of the families who have the children. It just makes me wonder—" Naomi paused mid-sentence.

"You wonder what?"

She sighed before she answered. "I wonder if they were really FBI."

"Come on, Naomi. You're getting paranoid."

"There was something not right about them. I'm scared. I'm really scared. What if they're out there, watching—waiting for us?"

"Did you give them the list?"

"Well, sort of. I gave them a list, but not the list."

"What? Are you crazy? So where is it?" he asked.

"Don't worry. I deleted it from my hard drive, and mailed a printout to someone I trust," she replied.

"Who? Why didn't you mail it to me?"

"Because you're in New Orleans! I had to get it away from here. I sent it to Mr. McClain at the camp. I trust him."

"So are you evacuating?"

"Yeah, the bus is almost here," she said.

"Bus? What do you need a bus for?"

"We've decided to gather up the children from the families they were temporarily staying with and evacuate together." Her brother was silent. "Hello? Did I lose you?"

"No. I'm here. Where are you taking them?"

"We don't know, yet. Still working on that," replied Naomi.

"OK. Listen, I have to go. You be careful, OK?"

"I will. You, too. I love you." There was no reply. The line went dead.

The Russian scientist sat at his desk browsing on his laptop at the latest report of Hurricane Katrina. Russian symphony music resonated in the large room. He pulled up a report on 15 Peruvian orphans who were recently sent to New Orleans when an email popped up.

Dr. Sokolov,

The 15 are on the move. Together. I don't know where to. What do you want me to do?

Dr. Sokolov sat back in his chair to think. He picked up his half-smoked cigar and took a few puffs. Then he put it back down and returned to his laptop.

I will take care of it from here. Stand by.

The doctor clicked "send" and then opened a new email. He typed:

To: Undisclosed

Subject: Take advantage of the storm

Body: We seem to be running into dead ends. United Adoption Agency keeps blocking. Now they have regrouped and are moving. This is our time to move—obtain the children. Do whatever it takes.

He clicked "send" and closed his laptop. Then he sat back in his office chair and puffed on his cigar. His gaze was on a framed picture of a beautiful blonde girl.

Monday, August 29, 2005. 8:14 AM. New Orleans, Louisiana

The sky was black as night. A massive chunk of building broke away and was lifted into the air. The large wooden and metal debris flew across the street and slammed into another building, crashing through a boarded up window of the business. Massive winds whipped mighty oaks on the boulevard, snapping many like toothpicks. It was hard to see due to the sheets of rain from the storm, and a violent wall of muddy water devoured up houses as it plowed into the city.

The gulf had shifted. Cars and trucks were rushing with the current; most of them had toppled upside down. Rooftops were being ripped off homes, revealing families hiding in the corners of their attics—parents shielding their children from the flying debris. Electric sparks popped as telephone poles snapped, pulling wires from their transformers.

The earth was angry, and the people who had survived its terror thus far were filled with a horrible fear. The meteorologists in New Orleans had painted a bleak picture for the future of the city, and now it seems their prediction was coming to pass.

Supplied with four milk jugs of water, a flashlight, and an axe, Rob Emanuel and his family were hunkered in the attic of their small home. The storm surge had unexpectedly pushed inland, and the Emanuels were one of many who had escaped from the rising water in their home. The children had never seen their father this scared, and Rob wanted nothing more than for his family's lives to be spared.

Max and Stella McClain sat on the edge of the seats in their living room watching on their television the storm's destruction of New Orleans. Their wide eyes and grim faces accurately portrayed the helpless feeling in their hearts for the people enduring the storm's wrath.

Max dialed a number on his cell. Busy signal. He tried again. Same thing. He tried one more time and, finally, got a ring. It rang a dozen times, but no one answered at the United Adoption Agency office in New Orleans. He looked at his wife and shook his head.

Rob swung his axe again and again and again, pounding the roof of his house from inside out. The water level from the surge was creeping higher and higher, and they could hear the sounds of the water rushing in below them and knocking their furniture around the small house. His children were crying, and his wife was trying to calm them. There wasn't much room for his backswing, but his axe finally bore a hole.

Just then, as if someone had turned on several spray nozzles, water began shooting up from the floor of the attic. Rob started swinging faster and faster, chipping away piece by piece the interior of his roof. The water level was rising fast in the attic, and the muscles in Rob's arms were burning. They were on their knees, and the water soon began to reach their chests. His children were screaming, and his wife was yelling his name!

Finally Rob made the hole just big enough for a person to squeeze through. He yelled for his wife to crawl through first, and then he helped his two kids through. Several minutes later, they were sitting on the roof of their home wondering what would happen next.

The sounds of the wind and rushing water from the gulf hurt their ears. It was nearly unbearable. Suddenly, Rob picked out the whipping of a helicopter approaching from the north. The Coast Guard had spotted them and was preparing to rescue the weary family.

Rob stood in the wind as best as he could, waving his hands to make sure the helicopter pilot saw them. The pilot hovered the chopper above the house, and the crew lowered a basket down to the roof. Rob helped his children inside first. He and his wife watched nervously as the basket was lifted upwards to the helicopter.

Suddenly, a blast of wind blew a chunk of debris straight toward the basket, knocking the basket sideways, and dumping their small son into the murky water. Rob and Christa screamed as they saw him fall.

Without hesitation Rob jumped into the water after his only son. The Coast Guard pulled up the little girl, and then they lowered the basket back down toward the spot where Rob jumped.

Christa was hysterical as she scanned the water for her husband and son. Suddenly, she saw Rob emerge and grab onto the basket with one hand. Then she saw their son. With one arm he hung onto the basket, and with the other he had a firm grip on his son. Rob wasn't about to let go of either. As if he had superhuman strength, he pulled his son out of the water and tossed him into the basket.

Rob hung onto the basket as it lifted him out of the water and back onto the roof of his house. Carefully, Rob helped his wife in, and the Coast Guard pulled them to safety. Then they finally retrieved Rob.

Now safely inside, Rob kissed his wife and kids as the helicopter flew them out of harm's way. He turned to look out of the chopper door and saw his house break from its foundation and crumble in the large, rushing waves of the Gulf of Mexico. With his children held tightly in his arms, he closed his eyes and cried.

Thursday, September 1, 2005. 3:02 PM

Squeaking brakes alarmed Stella as she looked toward the camp's entrance at the line of school busses pulling toward the office. The doors opened, and the weary and saddened people poured out, including the Emanual family. No one carried a suitcase, and most looked around as if they were lost.

Max McClain was in his camp office when he received the call that the authorities were sending evacuees from New Orleans to Camp Pinerock. Stella walked in as he hung up the phone. She informed him that six school busses of people just pulled in the campgrounds, and her husband revealed the reason for their arrival.

"OK," said Stella. "What do we do?"

"Are there many children on the busses?"

Stella sighed and looked intently toward her husband. "Just children with their families."

Max hung his head. Stella walked around behind him and placed her hands on his shoulders. "Still can't make any contact?"

"No. Nothing," answered Max.

"Honey, I'm sure—" She was interrupted by the sound of the front office door opening. Someone had just walked in.

"We better make some plans. I'll get on the phones, you start organizing our new campers."

"I'm on it," replied Stella with a smile on her face.

Thursday, September 8, 2005. 10:53 AM

Camp Pinerock was hosting over five hundred evacuees from New Orleans. Generous businesses and organizations had sent truck loads of supplies, and several Christians from area churches had sacrificed their time to sort all the supplies inside the camp's multipurpose building. A few more came to spend time, pray, and build friendships with the people. Nurses came to offer free healthcare, and police officers came to provide security.

The camp was near overload with almost every inch of space taken for sleeping. Rob and his family were safe, and their hunger was satisfied. Hurricane Katrina had stolen everything they owned. But they now had clothing, shelter, and someone who showed heartfelt devotion toward their physical, spiritual, and emotional needs.

Thursday, September 22, 2005. 5:24 PM

Two more weeks passed and the McClains were quite weary of the 24-hour dedication to the needs of the evacuees. However, they were also overwhelmed at the outpouring of supplies sent to help. They had recruited, organized, and delegated volunteers to cook, clean, watch children, life guard at the pool, as well as put out fights. There were lots of fights.

Christa Emanual had become good friends with Stella McClain. One afternoon the two were sitting on the porch of the

Director's house revisiting the frightening venture from Hurricane Katrina.

Stella had a personality that made people around her feel welcomed and relaxed. She was tenderhearted and soft-spoken. Her outer beauty reflected well the warmth of her inner charm.

Christa, especially, appreciated this. She needed this as her nerves were still shot. Her children still woke with nightmares about that day in the storm. But now she wanted something more that Stella seemed to possess. Something deeper than a personality. Christa couldn't figure it out, but she cherished her friendship with Stella.

Their conversation of the near-death experience grew to a calming silence as they rocked on the porch, appreciating the breeze of the late Southwest Louisiana afternoon. Stella broke the silence with a gentle question, "Christa, what are you trusting in to get to heaven?"

It was not an awkward question for Christa. Perhaps Stella realized Christa was dealing with the issue of trust, or maybe their conversation seemed to have led to this question. In any case, Christa felt the question was very appropriate and gave it some thorough thought before she answered.

"Stella, we were brought up to believe one thing, but—I don't know—now I seem to be questioning that. And I feel a bit guilty because of it."

"Do you feel guilt because you are asking questions? Or do you feel guilt because you have doubt?"

"Isn't that the same thing?" Christa asked.

"Not really. Asking questions means you want to know more. Doubting sometimes means you're already beginning to develop your conclusion. So, where are you?"

Christa looked toward the sunset—deep in thought over Stella's statement. She finally answered, "I want to know if it is possible for anyone to know for sure they will get to heaven. I've been told to believe that I have to make sure I live right, but I don't always live right. So how could anyone know for sure?"

Stella was impressed at the logic Christa had about the topic. So she asked another question, "Well, hasn't anyone ever taken a Bible and shown you how you can know for sure?"

Christa quickly glanced at Stella, then back to the sunset. She seemed somewhat frustrated as she answered, "No, Stella. No one has."

"May I?"

Christa turned back toward Stella. A smile formed on her face, and she nodded her head, "Yes. Please do."

The gym at the East Baton Rouge High School was loud and chaotic. Two weeks of sleeping bags on the gym's hardwood floor had made everyone cranky. Besides their fifteen Spanish-speaking boys and girls ages three to thirteen, many other families came to the high school gym for shelter. They all filled the place with playing, running, jumping, and lots of screaming. Naomi Kris seemed to have her composure under control despite the noise, but she could tell her wits were nearing their end.

Her head assistant, Rachel Willard, walked up holding one of the three year olds on her hip. "Naomi, we have to find somewhere else to go. I—I don't know how much more of this I can take."

"I know, I know. I can't take much more, either," agreed Naomi.

"Have you been able to reach your brother?"

"No, not yet. I still can't get through. It still goes straight to his voicemail."

"Naomi," said Rachel, "it doesn't mean anything bad happened. He's probably just at some shelter and doesn't know where you are." Rachel sat down next to Naomi and sat the little three year old girl on her lap. "Hey, listen. They're saying it will be at least two more weeks of no power here." Naomi just sat and stared at the children playing. A couple of volunteers had stayed behind to help the orphans.

Rachel continued, "There are places in Houston that are already housing evacuees. Maybe we oughta try. At least it would be a place with air conditioning."

"And how do you suppose we get there?" snapped Naomi.

Rachel leaned back in bewilderment. She had never seen Naomi this upset since her husband died two years ago.

"I'm sorry, Rachel." Naomi took in a deep breath. The air was stuffy and humid. "You have a good idea. We have to do something. We need transportation."

"It's OK. I'll get on it," replied Rachel with a smile.

Christa inhaled a chestful of the country air as she listened to Stella—someone who, finally, gave her the answers for which she had been searching. She felt a calming sense of relief. A strange and gentle peace surrounded her as she listened to her friend's words.

"It's a matter of bad news and good news, Christa. The bad news is about you and me, and the good news is about God," explained Stella. "The bad news is that you, me—well, everyone has sinned. We have all missed God's mark of perfection. The Bible says this in Romans 3:23. Here, read it." She opened a Bible and handed it to Christa who read the verse aloud.

"For all have sinned and have fallen short of the glory of God," read Christa. "What does that mean, though: fallen short?"

"We have missed God's mark. It's like if you and I were to try to throw a rock from here to New Orleans. Perhaps you could throw farther than I could, but neither one of us can make it. We miss it drastically—we fall short. That's the bad news, and it gets worse. Romans 6:23 tells us just how worse it gets. Here," Stella reached over to the Bible on Christa's lap and turned a few pages to the right. "Read this verse next."

Christa read aloud, "For the wages of sin is death."

"You know what wages are, right? It's what we earn at work, for example. The wages, what we earn, for our sin is death. This death is eternal separation from God. Wouldn't you say that is bad news?"

"Yeah. Pretty depressing," replied Christa.

"But here's where it gets good—for us. Turn to Romans 5:8." Christa flipped back a couple of pages in the Bible.

"But God demonstrated His own love toward us in that while we were still sinners Christ died for us." Christa looked up at Stella with a confused look on her face. "Why is this good news? Someone still died. This is what I never really understood. Why did Christ have to die?"

"That's a very good question, Christa. One that I used to have, as well. It's good news because He died for your sins and my sins. You and I are supposed to have paid for our sin by the death of Romans 6:23. But because of God's great love for you and me, He sent His only Son, Jesus, to pay the price for us.

"Let's say you have cancer, and it's terminal. I come to visit you one day and tell you that I can cure your disease. I can take it away, but I have to place it in someone else. So, I remove the cancer from you and place it in me. I die, but you live. I would be dying for you. It's the same with Jesus and us. He died instead of us. He paid for our sin so we wouldn't have to. And the good news gets better!"

Stella reached over and turned in the Bible to Ephesians 2:8. "Read these two verses."

"For it is by grace you have been saved, through faith—and this is not from yourselves, it is the gift of God— not by works, so that no one can boast," read Christa.

"Do you get it?" asked Stella. "Because Jesus paid for your sin—all of it—He offers you His everlasting life as a gift. It's a matter of trust or faith. Just like you are trusting in that rocking chair to hold you up, do you trust in Jesus that He paid for your sin and rose from the dead? It's not your good works that helps you get to heaven. His death, burial, and resurrection paid it all for you. Do you trust in Him?"

After so many years of wondering, Christa finally understood. Salvation wasn't something she did, but something God did. She realized she couldn't be saved from cleaning her act up, but by trusting in Jesus alone. And she did so in her rocking chair that afternoon.

Later that evening, Max was in his office answering emails when the phone rang. "Good afternoon, Camp Pinerock," he said.

"Hi. Is this Mr. McClain?" The quivering female voice was unfamiliar to Max.

"Yes ma'am, it is. How can I help you?"

"Mr. McClain, you don't know me. Uh, in fact, I'm not going to tell you who I am, but I just had to call to thank you for what you and your wife are doing at Camp Pinerock."

Max had received calls like this over the last month, but this one seemed different from the start. He replied, "Thank you, ma'am, for your encouragement. We appreciate your prayers."

"Mr. McClain, I am very angry," said the quivering voice. It took Max a couple of seconds to respond.

"OK..."

"It's not you. It's my church. Our pastor received a call asking if we could host a few families displaced by the hurricane. He immediately brought the need to our board, telling them that our church building would be the perfect place to host these families. But the board quickly rejected the idea, and our pastor just went with it."

Her voice grew from a quiver to near wrathful. Max just listened as she continued, "The request was to allow families to live in our Sunday school classes for a few weeks until they found permanent homes. But our leaders and most of our people are still against it! In fact, one of our deacons had the audacity to say that if we allowed someone to live in our classrooms, then we would not have a place to have Sunday School!"

Max's heart sank as he heard this news. He could hear the anger expounding from this woman. "Mr. McClain," she continued with a bit more control, "my church—instead of living like Christ by allowing destitute families use our classrooms as shelter—would rather use those rooms for forty-five minutes once each week to talk about living like Christ."

There was silence. Max was speechless. The voice remained quiet.

Finally, the woman calmly concluded, "I don't know what to do about this, but I had to vent. I heard of the work you and your team has been doing, and I just had to thank you for actually living out what you believe about Jesus—for living out the gospel."

Now it was Max who had a quiver in his voice. "I—I don't know what to say, ma'am. Thank you for your call. I know your passion and heartache. We couldn't do any of this without your prayers for us. Our God strengthens us. Your prayers for that strength are appreciated."

They ended the call, and Max sat stunned in his chair for several minutes. First, He battled his pride as he was tempted to tell himself he was such a great man for doing this great work, but then he turned to look out the window of his office and saw several of the children playing in the playground.

Then a distinct energy began to form inside—a burning that seemed to drive him to do something. There was an ache deep within his heart that could not be healed with anything less than sacrifice, sweat, tears, and devotion to the people of New Orleans staying at Camp Pinerock.

And he knew there were others. He knew that some out there in their sphere needed the help that he could give. This passion wasn't something he mustered up himself—it was something supernatural. This was from the Spirit of God. Then he prayed a wordless prayer—allowing the Spirit to speak for him.

Just a few days before, these children playing outside didn't know if they would survive that terrible storm. Now, they were safe in a place of love and peace. They were in a place that welcomed them, no matter what they looked like. And they were in a state of mind that was open to hear the truth about a Savior who gave His life for them. A tear formed in the eye of the camp director and trickled down his face.

Stella made a pot of coffee. It was time for a break, and she and Christa sat down in the living room. With her cup in one hand, Stella turned on the television. Christa was about to say something when her attention was drawn toward the screen. The news was describing another hurricane in the gulf that was fast approaching. The storm had already been named. Rita

CHAPTER TWO

Thursday, September 22, 2005. 6:23 PM

The bus cruised west on Interstate 10 loaded with the fifteen Peruvian children, Rachel, and Naomi. Rachel, sitting behind the driver's seat, leaned forward and asked the driver, "So what church is this bus from?"

"Terrance Road Presbyterian," answered the driver as Rachel sat back in her seat. "I've been the bus driver for about ten years now. Sure is a privilege to help y'all out, Ma'am!"

Somehow, Terrance Road Presbyterian Church received word that the children needed to be transported to another location and jumped on the opportunity to serve. Although the bus seemed quite used, Rachel and Naomi were grateful for the generosity and glad to be out of the stuffy high school gym.

Stella picked up her phone and called her husband next door at the camp office. Max, still gazing out his window pondering the conversation he just had with the woman, reached again for the ringing phone. Hearing the urgency in his wife's voice, his attention quickly switched into gear.

"Max, have you seen the news today?"

"No, why?"

"That tropical storm that hit Florida entered the gulf. It's now a major hurricane, and they're saying it is supposed to be heading this way." Stella paused for a response from Max and then continued, "Max? What should we do?"

Max's weary mind cranked back into gear. He let out a big sigh and then answered, "If it comes here, then we need to decide on where everyone should go." He thought for a few seconds and then looked toward the north. "The dining hall. It has a steel frame and should be sufficient to keep everyone safe."

"OK. Many have been relocated, so there are only about two hundred people here. We should have plenty of room for them to stay in the dining hall," responded Stella.

Max paused for a second as his mind worked. Then he said, "It's gonna be more than that, Babe."

"What do you mean?"

"There are families all around that will need to evacuate to the camp. There could be several hundred more."

Just then, two boys stormed in to Max's office.

"Mr. McClain, Mr. McClain," one of them shouted in a thick New Orleans accent. "My brutha be in a big fight! C'mon!"

Max quickly ended the call with his wife and rushed outside to see the large gathering of people circling the two brawlers. Two sheriff's deputies and a police officer were struggling to break up the crowd to get to the fighters. Max told the two boys to wait at the office and then ran to the fight. The crowd was shouting insults toward one another over the feud.

Max shoved his way inside the crowd, and as he apprehended one of the fighters he took an elbow straight to the mouth.

"Let me go, you #@%&!" shouted the boy. But when he noticed it was Max holding him, he calmed down. It was like a domino effect—the crowd silenced as each of them realized Max's presence. They stood staring at him, as if they were waiting on him to respond with the same violence they had shown.

Max said nothing, and they finally dissipated. The police officer walked over to Max and patted him on the shoulder as if to say "good job." Max wiped the sweat from his forehead with the arm of his sleeve, and the officer handed him a handkerchief. Max gave the officer a confused look, so the officer pointed to his mouth and said, "Looks like you got a bloody lip there, Max." He thanked him while wiping the blood from his mouth.

"It's been difficult tryin' to keep these two families apart. One member always seems to find a way to get at someone in the other family," said the policeman. "We might need more help with keeping the peace 'round here."

Max looked toward the south sky, "That's not all we'll need help with, Joe."

"You talkin' 'bout the hurricane comin'? Word's out it's a mighty big storm."

"Yeah, and there are many families around the area who live in houses that are likely not going to stand up to those high winds."

"Good point." The policeman looked around. "We'll need to evacuate the camp. Get everyone to a safe place."

"Actually, this is the safest place," said Max, wiping more blood from his lip.

"You're kiddin' me, right? A hurricane as strong as what they're sayin' Rita is 'll blow every one of these trees down. These buildings won't stand a chance."

"That dining hall is framed in steel, and there are no trees around it. The multipurpose building is on the south side of it. It'll take the worst of the wind, blocking it from the dining hall." Max looked at Joe and continued, "It'll work. It'll have to. There's no other option."

Stella and a couple of volunteers walked up to the two men as Max's cell phone rang. After a minute Stella saw the look on Max's face. She knew that look too well. He gave that expression when the wheels and cogs were working hard inside his mind—he was obviously formulating a plan.

"Sir, may I suggest an announcement be made that Camp Pinerock can be trusted as a shelter for everyone in the area. We have facilities suitable to withstand the storm." Max paused for a few seconds before continuing, "I don't see any other option. We have the largest buildings in the area to accommodate. And, yes, people can bring their small animals, too."

Max put his phone in his pocket and calmly explained the plan. "That was the mayor. We need to expect up to five hundred people arriving within the next twenty-four hours. Several will be bringing small animals: dogs, cats. They can be managed in the multipurpose building."

"What about all the extra food businesses have donated?" asked Stella. "If the storm cuts our power for any significant length of time—"

"Right," replied Max with raised eyebrows. "OK. Gather all perishable food items and store them in the dining hall's walk-in freezer. Tell everyone that the freezer door must stay shut as much as possible after the electricity goes out. All nonperishables need to be sorted and stored in the pantry."

Stella nodded and turned toward her two volunteers, "Go get everyone and meet me in the conference room for a quick meeting." The two volunteers hurried away to gather the others.

"Stella," Max said as he gently placed his hand on her shoulder, "the Gomez and Terrebonne families are at it again."

"I see that," said his wife as she licked her thumb and wiped the trickle of blood from his lower lip. "What do they hope to prove?"

"Who knows? But we have to keep them separated in the dining hall."

Stella thought for a few seconds and then exclaimed, "Why don't you just let me talk with the Gomez family, and you talk with the Terrebonnes? We can explain the situation to them, and how they have to keep to themselves during the storm."

"Good idea," said Max with a smile. His cell phone rang again—it was the Chief of Police. Max answered and made his proclamation, "Chief, I just spoke with the mayor. Camp Pinerock can be trusted as a safe haven from the storm. People can bring their pets, too. Make sure when you spread the word that you keep this message clear. Our facilities are strong enough to withstand the hurricane's high winds. People in our area should not try to stay home, but they should come here with as little belongings as they can."

8:36 PM

Most of the children were asleep on the bus, while Naomi was walking the aisle checking each child. With their stomachs full from the Happy Meals provided by Terrance Road Presbyterian Church, sleep came quickly. Naomi and Rachel enjoyed watching the children devour their cheeseburgers. Happy Meals were a long way away from what they were used to.

Naomi made her way to the front of the bus, and Rachel commented on how quiet it was after such a long day. Rachel leaned over to see little Isabella walk towards them. Isabella was a tiny four year old who hadn't spoken a word for the three weeks she had been in New Orleans. Her long, dark brown hair gently swung back and forth with the motion of the bus as she made her way to Naomi who reached under each arm and pulled her onto her lap.

"Como esta, Isabella? No puedes dormir? You can't sleep, hmmm?" asked Naomi. Isabella didn't answer. She just rubbed her eyes and snuggled with Naomi. Her petite frame was a delight to hold.

"Camp Pinerock isn't far from here," said Rachel. "I wonder how the McClains are."

"Me, too. They were supposed to meet with me tomorrow. He called me yesterday to see if he could check on the children. They're really excited about possibly adopting—"

Just then, the bus took a violent left turn on the interstate, and the driver yelled, "Hold on!" He had just noticed a black car whip in front of him, and someone throwing small objects out of the car. The bus' tires skidded on the pavement and leaned to one side. The driver screamed as he turned the wheel hard to the right to pull out of the skid, but it was no use.

The bus flipped onto its right side, shattering all its windows and tossing around its riders like ragdolls.

Darkness.

Just a few hundred miles away the sun was shining brightly through a massive hole in the sky. The edge of the hole reached upward to what seemed like several miles of a solid, gray wall with protruding masses of swirling, dark clouds. Suddenly, a reconnaissance aircraft broke through the wall and reported back to headquarters, "Maximum sustained winds are at 170 miles per hour, sir. We definitely have a Cat 5."

CHAPTER THREE

Friday, September 23, 2005. 6:30 AM

Max's eyes flickered open. He rolled out of bed and rubbed his face trying to wake up. His joints ached and cracked as he stretched, and his bottom lip was swollen. After a cup of black coffee and a banana, he headed out for his usual three-mile morning run.

Chris Sonnier was already awake. He was outside with a hammer in one hand and a nail in another boarding up the windows of his family's old house. Sarah, his wife of six years, opened the front door and walked onto the porch. She had a cup of piping, hot coffee in one hand and hot decaffeinated tea on the other. "Chris, Mom wants us to come out to her house," she said.

"Ha! I'm not about to drive all the way up to Oklahoma. No, we're gonna ride it out right here at home," Chris replied while gathering another handful of nails.

Sarah held out the cup of coffee toward her husband as she sipped hers. Then she said, "Well, actually, I want us to go to Mom's, too. This is not a typical thunderstorm, Chris. They're saying it's already a Category 5."

Chris sat his hammer down, took the cup from his wife's hand, and sipped the piping, hot coffee before his reply. "Honey, this isn't the first hurricane this house has withstood. Trust me; you don't wanna be stuck in all that traffic! Remember Katrina just a few weeks ago? There was a surge of people filling up every road out of New Orleans." He took another sip, and then he said, "Besides, as many times as you have to go to the bathroom every hour—" He smiled as he looked at her beach ball-shaped midsection.

"Perhaps you're right," replied Sarah with a deep sigh. Then she clarified herself, "About the house withstanding, that is."

She was seven months pregnant with their second child—a girl. Their first, Jeffery, just turned four years old the day before, and party streamers and balloons still hung around the dining room.

"Anyway," continued Chris as he picked up his hammer and maneuvered another nail between his fingers, "the message I got from ol' man John next door was that we all should stay in our own homes. There's nowhere else for us to go around here."

Sarah was worried, but didn't want to go against Chris. The last thing she needed was to start off the day with another fight. She turned around, walked back into the house, and murmured to her husband, "I'm goin' to take a shower."

Cars and trucks began to fill up the camp's parking lot. Volunteers from nearby homes and churches were directing the coming people into the large dining hall. It was mid-morning and Stella was supervising the volunteers and staff in the dining hall's kitchen.

Max walked in. He was on his cell, which was not unusual for the last two days, but this time his voice expressed frustration.

Stella waited until he finished before speaking up, "What's wrong?"

"I just got a call from Mike Sage," he said while putting his phone in his back pocket.

"The new pastor at First Baptist?"

"Yes." Max paused and stared at Stella as if to emphasize his frustration.

"What's wrong? Is he OK?"

"He asked where we were going to escape the hurricane. He asked if we wanted to ride it out at his house."

"At his house? He should be coming here! I thought everyone was supposed to be receiving calls from the city's office to come here." Then Stella realized the problem. "Max, that means some are getting the wrong message," she said in a lowered voice. "We have to do something. Most of these homes are very old—they won't stand up to 100 mile per hour winds."

"I told him to begin making calls to everyone he knows in the area."

"Why don't we just call the city to tell them they're sending out mixed messages?"

"Mike tried that," said Max. "He couldn't get through—all the lines are busy. We need some of our available staff to divide the area into territories to begin making calls. Put Josh in charge. He knows the area pretty well."

"Max, most of our staff and volunteers are tied up with other duties. There's hardly anyone left for this." Max took a deep breath. Then he started looking around.

"I have an idea," he said.

Many of the wild animals in the woods surrounding the area innately realized the coming of something big, and a family of raccoons had sought shelter underneath the Sonnier's house. Most of the houses in the old, country town sat on short concrete piers. Sometimes, skunks would nest underneath a house, causing an eye-watering stench to seep through the floor.

The Sonnier's home was about sixteen inches off the ground, and out of curiosity, one of the raccoons began playing with an old wire hanging a few inches from the bottom of the floor of the house. Then, to his demise, the raccoon bit the wire. A rush of electricity jolted through his little body causing sparks to fly everywhere. Then the lifeless animal laid still with smoke gently rising upwards.

The wire had become separated from the floor and hung near some steel tubing stashed underneath the wooden house. Chris didn't hear the popping noise because of his hammering, and Sarah was in the shower.

They also didn't hear the weatherman on the television give his latest report of Hurricane Rita. If they could've heard him, they would have realized that Caroline Springs sat in the center of the storm's path, and the winds were expected to be sustained at over 130 miles per hour.

All seemed quiet and dark. Then a gentle light formed. And faint sounds of people talking.

She couldn't make out what they were saying, but the talking was getting louder. She tried to open her eyes, but they were so heavy. She could tell that people were all around her, but she didn't know where she was.

Finally, Rachel opened her eyes and noticed her world was on its side. A hand reached out to her. Then a voice, "Ma'am! Ma'am, are you OK? Can you hear me?" The hand touched hers, and she gently grabbed it.

"What happened? Where am I?" she asked.

"You were in a bus accident. Here, let me help you." The man carefully began to guide Rachel toward him. She realized he was reaching in through a hole in the roof of the bus. She crawled on her other hand and knees through the hole.

With the help of three people, Rachel stood to her feet. The world was spinning, and she tried to recall the incident.

The violent jerking of the bus. The children! Isabella! Naomi!

Rachel became frantic, yelling for Naomi and the children. She began to lose control of her legs, and her head felt like it was swimming. A few people who had gathered around her helped her sit down. Everything was chaotic. She heard sirens. Lots of sirens. More people and more talking. She heard authorities barking out orders.

Two paramedics quickly approached her and began their work. Rachel was confused and terrified. Her world suddenly seemed very empty, very dark, and petrifying.

CHAPTER FOUR

Friday, September 23, 2005. 4:45 PM

There was an eeriness at Camp Pinerock. One could almost smell the fear rising from the campgrounds. The wind was beginning to pick up, and dark, swirling clouds were hovering just a few thousand feet in the sky. Rumblings of thunder could be heard in the distance from the south.

The Katrina evacuees seemed the most fearful, and rightly so—they had already been through this horrific ordeal. But Max, Stella, and their team were steady calming them—giving hope, peace, and encouraging them to keep their thoughts on Jesus Christ.

Already a few of the Katrina evacuees were bonding with the newcomers from the surrounding area. Although their skin color and accents were different, their commonality of the situation had caused multiple conversations to transform into immediate friendships.

Stella put Josh Ward, the Assistant Director, in charge of recruiting volunteers to call people in different areas of the old town. As was Max's idea, they were given clear direction to make their way quickly to the camp, but Josh and his team had little success in calling those who received the wrong message. It was hit and miss, and Josh felt he was wasting his time. He walked in to Max's office to share his frustration.

"This isn't working, Max," vented Josh.

"Talk to me." Max was sitting at his desk jotting down notes on a legal pad.

"Most of the people we're calling either already know about coming here, or they've already made their way. I feel we could be doing something better than this." Max sat back in his chair, took off his reading glasses, and thought for a minute.

"Tell me about the ones you contacted who got the wrong message."

"What do ya mean? What about 'em?"

Max sat forward in his chair. "Are there any similarities?"

Josh thought for a minute. His passion for reaching these isolated folks was obvious. In fact, his passion for people had grown significantly.

His parents were killed in a car wreck when he was 3, and he was passed around from foster home to foster home until he was adopted by a couple who already had two kids of their own.

His new parents were loving, but he wrestled with acceptance and trust for several years, wondering if anyone cared—if anyone ever noticed his anguish and desperation for attention. He trusted in Christ when he was 10 years old at a Good News Club put on by Child Evangelism Fellowship at his public school. In time these emotions grew fixed on Christ, and his passion for helping people when life's traumas became intense.

Acquiring these people who were in danger and in dire need of help was Josh's highest ambition. He thought about the similarities as his boss had asked.

"They're all old," Josh said with one raised eyebrow. "They're all retired elderly people." Max picked up his phone and called the mayor to explain what they had discovered.

The dining hall was filling up quickly, and the noise level was rising. The staff and volunteers were organizing the families into different sections of the large hall, while other volunteers were bringing in cots, mattresses, and blankets from the cabins.

Max and Josh burst through the front doors and made their way to one of the staff leaders. Max explained the situation—that people were needed to head out into parts of town to rescue the elderly. The staff leader informed them that everyone was tied up helping the incoming people.

Max walked to the dining hall's stage, turned on the hall's sound system, and picked up the microphone. "May I have your attention? May I have your attention, please?"

The noise of the crowd settled, and Max continued, "My name is Max McClain. I'm the Director, here, at Camp Pinerock, and I need your help. We are very glad that y'all are here, but we have a problem which needs immediate action. We just found out there are many elderly people still in their homes. Apparently, they received the wrong message from the city's office. That message was to stay in their homes.

"Obviously, they are in danger. I just spoke with the mayor who is trying his best to be on top of the situation. However, he informed me that these folks are unable to get here on their own. So this is where you come in. I realize it's getting worse out there each minute, but we need several of you to volunteer to drive to their homes and bring them here. Please know that this could be dangerous, but your assistance could save lives."

"Are you crazy?" someone shouted. "That storm jus' 'bout on us!"

"How many people we tawkin 'bout?" someone else asked in a thick Cajun accent.

Max responded, "We are still getting the total number in, but we believe there are at least eighty to as many as a hundred and twenty. Time is not on our side."

"Do you have maps?"

"Yes, we have maps for everyone." Max continued, "If you would like to volunteer, please follow me to our camp office."

Suddenly, lightning struck just outside the dining hall, and the heart-stopping thunder made everyone jump. Max quickly turned off the sound system. When he turned back toward the crowd, he saw a large number of people exit the front door of the dining hall and head for the camp office.

Josh stepped up and said, "Well, you asked for more help. Looks like you got it." He patted Max on the back and headed out the door.

Max walked into the foyer of the camp office when Stella approached, "What did the mayor say?" Max breathed in deeply before he answered. "The list of the town's people they divided among the city office's staff was according to age, not alphabetical order. There was an employee who interpreted the interoffice memo wrong. He was telling the people on his list not to come to the camp, but to stay home. On his list were people seventy-five years and older."

Stella's eyes were wide due to her disbelief that something so important as this message could be so easily misread. Max checked his cell phone and concluded, "He just emailed me the list. We have everyone's address who received the wrong message."

"How many?" Max was silent. Stella repeated herself, "Max, how many?"

"Two hundred and ten."

"Oh God, help us!" Stella covered her mouth with her right hand in disbelief. "But what about the city? What are they doing about it?"

"They have already closed the office. Everyone is leaving town. The mayor included."

Max and his wife walked into the large conference room where everyone had gathered. A volunteer came in with a stack of photocopied maps and several yellow highlighters. Max picked up a highlighter and instructed everyone to watch and listen.

With a map on the table and all sixty people gathered around as best as they could, Max drew a large circle on the map and explained, "This is the area we are targeting. Here is the camp in the center of the circle. Each of you will be on a team to quickly drive out to a home and bring back the evacuee and a few of his or her belongings. Very few! This could include pets. Stella will assign the teams and hand each team a slip of paper with an address on it. I want you to use the highlighter to draw the same circle as you see on my map, and then mark your line following the route from the camp to the person's home you are heading to."

"You want us to find our radius," interrupted one of the new volunteers.

"Pardon me? I don't follow," replied Max.

"I apologize," said the volunteer. "I'm a math teacher. What you are asking is for us to find our radius from the camp to the where the evacuee lives."

Max smiled. "No apology necessary. That's exactly what I'm asking." Then he said to the rest of the crowd, "Thank you all for your help. Please listen to Stella as she assigns teams and hands out the maps and highlighters. Each of you must find your radius quickly," said Max as he nodded at the math teacher. Then when Stella was finished, he prayed with the teams before they headed out.

In a matter of minutes, each team left to follow its radius, including Max. As they were driving off, the tall pine trees began to bend with the increasing strength of the wind.

Thirty miles south of the camp, Lake Charles Memorial Hospital was on high alert. In addition to the normal capacity, the ER hosted several children, Naomi and Rachel, and a large team of doctors and nurses scrambling around each other.

Rachel sat on her bed in disbelief while watching the commotion of the medical staff hard at work. One of the nurses was bandaging her right shoulder that was cut by glass. Rachel asked the difficult question that had been in her mind for the last half hour, "What about the children? Are they all OK?"

The nurse gave her a quick look, and then went back to her bandaging. Rachel pleaded, "Please. Tell me."

The nurse finished her bandage, looked through the door of the room, and then back to Rachel. Then she said, "I'm not supposed to talk about this right now. I'm sorry." With that, the nurse left the room.

Rachel watched with bewilderment as the nurse exited the room. Nausea pained her stomach, and she buried her head in her hands and prayed and cried.

CHAPTER FIVE

Friday, September 23, 2005. 6:33 PM

The sky was getting darker by the minute, and the winds were picking up fast. An old Ford F-150 drove down a gravel driveway up to an old, white two-story house. Charlie Metcalf and his son, Rog, got out of the truck and walked up the steps of the front porch. They had never been down this road before.

"Who lives here?" asked Rog.

Charlie looked at the slip of paper that Stella had given him at the camp. "Ms. Velma Hannicut." Charlie stepped up to the front door and knocked 4 times. "Ms. Hannicut?" he yelled.

Suddenly, the door slowly glided open about 10 inches, giving off an eerie squeal. "OK," said Rog. "That was weird."

Charlie began to walk inside as his son protested, "Dad! We can't just go inside. That's breaking and entering"

"What did we break, son?" his dad replied shrugging his shoulders. "Besides, we have to make sure she's OK—if she's here at all." Charlie looked to see if anyone was around, and then the two burley men walked inside the house, calling out the elderly lady's name.

"This place gives me the creeps," stated Rog. The wind made awful whistling noises that made Rog's hair rise on the back of his neck, and the old house cracked and groaned. They walked down a long hall that had dark rooms on both sides. Charlie tried to switch on a light, but nothing happened. "The power must be out already."

They came to a set of stairs, but Rog insisted they leave. "Son, she might be asleep or something. We have to make sure," exclaimed his dad.

"Come on, Dad. This house is freakin' me out. If she was asleep, she would've heard us calling her name by now."

"What's the matter?" asked his dad as he turned to face his son. "You scared, or somethin'?"

Rog gave his dad a smirk. "Wha—? Na—no! I'm not scared, but we're wasting our time—"

Just then, Charlie saw something dash across the hall behind Rog. His eyes widened with sudden fear, and Rog quickly pranced over to his dad's side.

"What! What was it? Dad, you'd better not be messin' with me!"

"Shhhh! Be quiet," whispered his dad. "Someone's in the house."

"What? What did you see? Come on, Dad. Let's just go! It's not like there's a hurricane comin', or anything!"

"It was a dark figure. I dunno—maybe 6 feet tall, or somethin'," Charlie estimated. They were whispering as if not to awaken something evil.

The two men sat quietly for a minute, looking around for anything unusual. "Do you think it was a person?" asked Rog.

"No," remarked his dad calmly. He paused before he answered, "I think it was a cat. A six-foot-tall cat." Now Charlie had the smirk on his face.

Rog stared at his dad with big, brown eyes, inhaled deeply, and asked, "Was it a black cat?"

Charlie slowly turned his head toward his son. "You're 24 years old, you know!" he whispered loudly. Just then, the floor creaked, and both men bolted their gaze toward the sound. Then, to their horror, they saw a strange figure lurking from one room to the next. It seemed to float by with ease, but because the lights were out it was too difficult to make the figure out.

Rog began to shiver. Charlie looked around to see if he could find something—anything he could use as a weapon. The only thing he could find was a pair of women's dress shoes with high heels. He picked them up, and Rog commented, "I don't think that's your color, Dad."

"Shut up." The two men quietly tip-toed down the hall toward the front door. They couldn't see the figure, but they heard a noise. It sounded like chains jingling.

"Alright," Rog said out loud. "I am officially freaked out." Apparently mustering up a high level of bravery, he stood up tall and walked sternly toward the sound of the chains.

"Rog! Get back here!" Charlie whispered loudly.

"No, this is ridiculous," blurted his son. Rog turned a corner to his left and, suddenly, the dark figure jumped out from a shadow onto Rog's back!

Rog screamed out like a little girl, whipped around in circles and tried to get the figure off his back. Charlie ran over and started beating the figure with a size seven—one in each hand—except once he accidently whacked his son in the head, which caused his son to become quite angry.

Rog threw himself backward and slammed the figure against the wall. Just then, the power came back on. All the lights were beaming, and the father and son tag team could finally see their opponent.

"Branson!" shouted both men.

"What are you doing here?" yelled Charlie.

The thin man, dressed in all black, stuttered before he gave his answer. "W— w— why are you beating me with women's shoes?" Charlie looked at the shoes in his hands, and then back at Branson who was rubbing his back where he was beaten. Then he raised one shoe in an attempt to hit him again.

"Check this out, Dad," said Rog. He picked up a bag full of jewelry and other loose items. "He's robbing Ms. Hannicut!"

"Alright," said Charlie, "you're coming with us. We have two more people to pick up. Everyone else is already back at the camp. Let's go." Charlie and Rog each grabbed one of Branson's arms and dragged him to the front door. Branson protested as he was being dragged.

"If Ms. Hannicut was here she probably would have shot you!" shouted Rog.

They paused before going through the doorway, and Charlie looked at Branson and said, "Idiot."

Friday, September 23, 2005. 11:42 PM

The darkness was suffocating, and there were two-, sometimes three-toned sounds of eerie minor keys that, at times, clashed and other times harmonized with each other.

Occasionally, one particular sound produced enough resonance to cause massive vibrations to fill the entire black atmosphere of the enormous room. Two hours of the most horrific howls filled the multipurpose building at the camp.

Josh and a crew of nine staff and volunteers were managing the animals in the large building. Most of the dogs were howling along with the wind, and as the time went by, the wind noise began to drown out the howling of the dogs.

The same sounds were frightening the Sonnier's, as well. Chris had boarded up most of the windows. This provided an opportunity for the wind to create eerie whistles and high-pitched screams. To Sarah the sounds were like a woman's screams of terror.

She held her son as the family hunkered down inside the master bedroom's walk-in closet. Chris checked his watch. It was 11:45p.m., and stomachs were in tight knots while ears were sore from the loud sounds. They could hear trees snapping and timber falling just outside.

Chris' nerves were near splitting. He wished they had left. Guilt was flooding his mind as he looked at his pregnant wife and son and the fearful countenances they displayed on their faces. His thoughts drifted, perhaps in order to calm his emotions.

From the depths of his mind he heard an old, familiar tune coming from his dad's barn. He missed his dad and the old 50's music he used to blare from the radio in the barn. He missed the way his dad would take great interest in his favorite hobby—playing his fiddle in his Blue Grass band. Even though his dad was severely tone-deaf, he loved listening to his son play.

Every Saturday night Chris' band would play for hours while friends and family would come and enjoy the music, laughter, and food. But that stopped three years ago when his dad passed away from a heart attack.

Chris could see lights shining through the windows of the old barn, and silhouettes of people dancing. He could hear the sirens from the ambulance. He saw his dad in the hospital bed in the emergency room, and he could smell the aromas from the supplies and equipment the medical team used to try to revive Mr. Sonnier.

The doctors and nurses were slowly walking out of the room as Chris cautiously made his way in. They looked at him with sorrowful faces. Chris stood beside his father's body.

Then he saw a dark road—the road he drove to leave his sadness and anger behind. He drove fast and far. He didn't realize he was driving further into his sadness and anger.

From that time on, Chris emotionally and physically drove away from almost everyone in his life. Other than Sarah and Jeffery, he had no friends by his own choosing. And Sundays were no longer spent in the company of other Christians who were meant to console and encourage him.

Then his senses suddenly brought him back to reality.

He smelled smoke.

Inside the dining hall young children cried as they were consoled by their parents. Each family had one mattress where they could rest during the storm, but no one was asleep. The power had been out for over an hour, and all the perspiring people packed inside produced a sticky heat that was taking its toll on their noses.

Max checked in with Josh on his radio, who confirmed all was well. But Josh didn't feel well. Max had tried to comfort him earlier by stating that the multipurpose building was made with the same steel as the dining hall was. "But it's much bigger," Josh answered in his mind. "More for the wind to damage."

"Is that a—a jet?" yelled one of the volunteers. The sound above grew extremely loud.

"Josh, that sounds like a jet plane overhead!" shouted another.

Josh looked up, and then they all covered their ears at the deafening scream from above. Suddenly, Josh felt a vibration in his pocket. He pulled out his cell phone and saw a name appear that he hadn't seen in almost 3 years. "Chris?" he shouted as he covered his other ear.

"Jo—! –osh! Can—hear—?" Josh could barely hear blips of Chris' voice.

"Chris! You're cuttin' out!" Josh yelled as best he could above the storms screams.

"—osh! –house is—"

"What? Repeat!"

"My—on fire! My house is on fi—Sarah—Jeffery—" Josh's phone lost its signal.

Chris dashed back toward the burning house from his truck. Horrible panic had overtaken his thoughts and stolen his breath. He didn't know what to do. He tried to call Josh again, but he couldn't get through.

His chest severely tightened as he ran around to the back of the house. The fire had overtaken the entrance. He shouted with every ounce of energy he possessed, "SARAH! JEFFERY!" Chris was sobbing enormously as he shouted again, "SARAH!"

Suddenly, the sound of a fast approaching freight train drew from behind, and a violent blast of wind exploded through a stack of firewood. The blast blew the wood and debris right into Chris, tossing him like a ragdoll several feet away. His eyes rolled back in his head as he fell to the ground.

Max and Stella were sitting together on the stage in the corner of the dining hall. The tremendous winds were frightening most of the children, but at least they were all safe. Stella looked at her husband proudly and expressed as much to him with a kiss on his cheek.

Max looked at his bride and smiled. Stella smiled back and said, "You do know what we were planning to do tomorrow, right?"

Max breathed deeply and replied, "Yeah. We were going to visit one of the families with hopes of adopting a little Peruvian girl. I don't think we'll make it tomorrow, do you?" Max sheepishly grinned at Stella.

Stella laid her head on his shoulder—her mind drifting back over the last 15 years of their marriage. She frowned a bit when her thoughts came to the fact that they were never able to have children. She reminisced about how they came to Camp Pinerock. After Max's early retirement from the FBI, they became directors of the camp. Camp life provided plenty of opportunities to invest in the lives of children; and invest, they did. But they longed for a child of their own.

For the last two years, they prayed about adopting. When they found out that Josh was adopted out of the United Adoption Agency in New Orleans, they had made arrangements to make a visit on Saturday of that week.

Stella always wanted a little girl she could spoil with pretty pink dresses and tea sets. She fantasized about adopting, and Max couldn't wait to make the visit. His heart was broken that they were not able to have a child, but God had given them a great sense of peace about the adoption process.

The UAA had an impeccable reputation. He was looking forward to the visit. Why did God change plans? Or did He?

Stella noticed her husband's face grow dim, and she knew why. Her husband was always strong. His tall, athletic frame and take-charge personality was what attracted her to him. Yet, he also had a compassionate side—a side that was eager to honor God and love people.

He served his God and country with tremendous sacrifice. Not many knew of his expeditions over the years with the military and FBI. Not many could. She realized that even she didn't know most of what he had endured.

She always looked at her husband with admiration, and now she looked at him with compassion. "I'm sure they are all fine, honey," she said. He smiled at his bride, and then put his arm around her and held tightly.

"Just a little more! A little more! Almost there!" Two young men pushed hard on the door exposing them to the violent wind. Finally, it was open far enough for Josh to squeeze through and run into the storm toward the dining hall. The two buildings were close enough to each other to produce a breezeway that funneled the strong, hurricane-force winds.

He worked hard to keep his balance as the wind whipped between the two buildings, but they were too strong. Like a giant hand, the wind picked Josh up off his feet and dropped him hard on the pavement. He managed himself back to his feet and stooped head first into the wind toward the dining hall. He marched as if he was pushing a large boulder. Then he burst through the front doors and yelled for Max, who immediately jumped to his feet and came running toward him.

"What's the matter?" said Max. "What happened? You're bleeding!" He pointed to Josh's bleeding elbow from the blast he just received, but Josh wasn't interested in telling that story.

Trying to catch his breath, Josh held out his cell phone and answered, "I just got a call from Chris Sonnier. It was sketchy, but he's apparently at his house. I heard him say fire, then Sarah and Jeffery!"

"What? They stayed home?" said one of the volunteers as he jumped into the conversation.

"We have to go get 'em, Max. We have to go now," continued Josh in between deep breaths.

One of the staff members stepped up and interrupted the conversation. "Wait, wait! We don't know where they are! We can't go out in this storm!"

Josh gave a daring look at the protester and forcefully replied, "He said the words house, fire, and his family—what more do you want to know?"

Max intervened, "Alright, calm down. We'll get a team together and head out." Then he turned towards everyone else who eagerly wanted to know what was going on. "We have an emergency situation, but we'll handle it. Just stay calm. The storm will soon be over."

Just as Max turned to walk away, one of the Katrina evacuees stood up. "What's the emergency?"

"Grant," said Max as he packed his backpack with tools, "I said don't worry about it. We'll handle it."

"Mr. McClain, I'm not tryin' to start any trouble. I just wanna help."

Grant's cousin spoke up, "G, you can't go out there! Sit down!"

"Shut up! You should be comin', too!" shouted Grant.

"You know what, Grant? I could use your help," said Max. "Thanks for volunteering." Josh gave a questioning look toward Max, but said nothing.

"I'm coming, too." Everyone's attention turned towards another evacuee who was standing to his feet. Tossing his backpack over his shoulder, Max walked over to him and quietly spoke. "Daniel, I just broke up a fight between you and Grant. You actually jacked me in the jaw. What makes you think I'm gonna let you help?"

"I'm sorry, Mr. McClain." Daniel Gomez hung his head and then looked up. "I wanna make up for it. Please let me come help. I promise not to start anything."

"Let him go, Mr. McClain," said Daniel's mother.

Max thought for a couple of seconds, and then walked over toward Grant's family. Josh called out, saying they had to leave.

"Mrs. Terrebone?" said Max to Grant's mother. He paused for an answer.

"He needs to do this. It would be good for him to do somethin' worthwhile for a change." Mrs. Terrebone gave Grant a sturdy look and continued, "It's time he do somethin' good for someone else."

Max paused before giving his answer, "Fine. Let's go. Josh—grab a couple of guys and meet me at the truck."

Chris was going in and out of consciousness. He couldn't tell if he was dreaming or not, but as he tried to open his eyes he could barely make out a familiar sound. Someone was calling his name. Immediately, he heard the bluegrass music playing in the barn. "Chris! Chris, where are you?"

Chris tried to sit up. "Dad? Dad, I'm here! I'm over here!" Chris' head injury from the blast of firewood caused severe pain, and he was about to pass out again before he saw bright lights.

Chris could barely make out the blurry-looking flashlights coming toward him. "Chris! Are you OK?" Josh knelt down while trying to protect himself from flying debris. He saw blood on Chris' forehead and left shoulder. Josh helped him to his feet toward the large Dodge 4x4 truck.

The others ran toward the burning house, but Grant stopped. Guarding his face with his forearm, he tried to look at the house. Max quickly surveyed the situation. There was a giant pine tree lying horizontal in the middle of the house, and flames were shooting upwards and whipping around with the violent wind.

"Go around back!" shouted Max. The hurricane's eyewall was approaching. One hundred fifteen mile-per-hour winds were heading right toward them.

As the men ran around the back, Max stopped and yelled, "Right here! Everyone, come here!" The men met him at a broken window of the house. "Help me remove the rest of the glass. Then I'll climb in and look for Sarah and Jeffery!"

They quickly searched for something on the ground they could use to break off the rest of the glass from the bottom of the window. Limbs and debris were blowing all around them. Grant caught a small limb and went to work on the window. When they removed the glass, Max started to jump up, but he was held back by two hands.

"Mr. McClain! You can't do this!" It was Daniel. "You'll get burned!"

"Daniel, let go—I have to! They'll die if I don't," replied Max.

"But you might die! How do you know you won't die?" Just then a massive gust of wind nearly blew both men over to the ground. Max had a firm grip on the window seal and grabbed Daniel with his other hand to steady him back to his feet.

"I don't, Daniel! But I have to try! This is when we have to be courageous! This is the moment we trust in God; He hasn't left us, Daniel!" Max looked into Daniel's eyes which were watering from either the wind or fear. "He's here—right here! You wait for me! Hang on to the window seal!"

"What are you going to do?"

"I don't know! I'll figure it out when I get inside!"

Daniel removed his grip from Max's shoulders, and Max jumped up, pulled himself through, and crawled on his knees to stay underneath the smoke. Flashing light from flames came from all directions, but Max kept crawling and calling out for Sarah.

Moments later Grant heard Max yell for him. He looked into the window and saw Max crawling while carrying little Jeffery in one arm. "Daniel! Guys! Help me get the boy!"

The others came and pulled Jeffery out the window. One of them carried him to a vehicle. Max saw Jeffery coughing, and he immediately crawled back into the burning house.

Suddenly, there was a loud crash. Sparks, flames, and smoke shot upward like a volcano. Then they started twisting into a funnel of fire whipping around like a bull whip. The window was inaccessible. Daniel, Grant, and the other men could hear a yell come from inside the house.

"That sounded like Max!" shouted one of the men.

Daniel grabbed Grant's arm, the two ran to another window a few yards down from where Max had climbed through. "Help me break away the glass!" shouted Daniel.

When they cleared the broken glass away, Daniel yelled, "Help me through!"

Grant froze for a second before responding, "Are you sure?"

"Yeah! I'm sure! Help me through!"

Grant interlocked his fingers for Daniel's foot and helped him up towards the window. Daniel climbed through and landed on his back. He rolled over onto his hands and knees and squinted his eyes to see. The smoke was thick just over his head. He began crawling and shouting out for Max.

Grant yelled from outside, "You see anything?" But he heard no reply. The wind noise was far too loud.

Josh was cleaning the wounds of his friend inside the big diesel truck. Suddenly, Chris woke and sat up with a shout. "Sarah! Jeffery!"

Josh had to restrain him. "Chris! Chris! Max is getting them now! You have to lie still—you're bleeding everywhere!" Chris laid back down. His breathing was heavy, but he managed to speak a few more words.

"Josh. Josh, get Dad. Dad is out there." His eyes were closed, but he kept talking. "Josh, Dad called out to me. He's out there. We have to help him."

Josh realized Chris was delusional, so he spoke calmly to help him relax. "Chris, settle down. You have to relax." Josh looked out the window toward the burning house and prayed, "God, help us."

Rachel couldn't contain herself. After seeing Naomi in her room, hooked up to 3 monitors and a couple dozen wires, she had to find out about the children. The hospital's backup generators kicked on, and doctors and nurses were all over the place.

Finally, she reached out her hand and grabbed the sleeve of one of the E.R. doctors. "Sir, please, I must know about the children. They are all orphans from a village in South America. Please tell me. Please!"

The doctor saw the desperation in her eyes. "Ma'am, I'm very sorry, but we were told not to discuss with anyone the matter of the orphans."

"Those orphans are my responsibility!" Rachel shouted.

The doctor could tell that in her determination she wasn't about to let go of his sleeve. Plus, the doctors all marveled at the children, and he wanted answers, too. He looked around and then replied, "OK. Come with me."

She followed him into a small medical supply closet and closed the door behind him. She was very confused about the secretiveness of this discussion. She wondered why they had to be in private for him to tell her the news—whether it was bad or good.

"Um—the children," he began. "We really are baffled at this. This was quite an accident—involving a lot of broken glass—many children. We—we can't explain it."

"Explain what?" she interrupted.

"Most of the children—" The doctor shook his head in disbelief and removed his glasses. "We're monitoring them right now. Ma'am they haven't a single scratch on them. No bruises. No broken bones—nothing." The doctor looked intently into Rachel's eyes. "They're all OK. Where did you say you were going? What can you tell me about these kids?"

Rachel didn't respond to his questions. She covered her mouth with her hands—her eyes wide and bright. Then she dropped her hand and said, "They're not hurt? You mean—they're really OK?"

"Yes. They are fine. Well, all—but one."

"What? Who? Which one? You must take me to see!"

The doctor sighed with a sense of frustration. He had many questions. He opened the door and exited the closet. Rachel followed closely behind.

They turned a corner and walked through a set of double doors. She could hear the beeping of computers and monitors. Rachel's heart was full of anxiety. She followed him into a room where she saw a little girl with her head wrapped in gauze. She had wires on almost every appendage. Rachel's eyes filled with tears as she gazed upon the girl lying in the bed. It was Isabella.

The doctor turned to Rachel and said, "The other 10 are in perfect condition. This is the only child who was hurt. We think she'll be just fine, though."

Rachel turned to the doctor and blurted out in confusion, "Ten? We have fifteen children!"

"Mr. McClain! Mr. McClain! Where are you?" Daniel had trouble breathing but kept going. Finally, he heard a shout.

"Over here!" Max strained to yell. Daniel crawled around a corner and found him with Sarah. She had passed out, and Daniel noticed a lot of blood coming from Max's side.

"What happened?" shouted Daniel. He managed his way closer and realized what caused Max to yell out. He was in a tight plank position with Sarah underneath him and a huge beam resting on his back. Max had kept the beam from crushing her, and he somehow had enough strength to hold the beam up with his back. As Daniel reached for Sarah's hand to pull her to him he noticed what had caused Max to bleed. A nail had sliced open a six inch gash in his left side.

"Pull her out!" yelled Max. Daniel carefully dragged her to the window.

"Grant! Help me!" shouted Daniel from just inside the house. Grant yelled for the other men to come help.

After a couple of minutes, they got Sarah out safely and to the truck, but Daniel was still in the house. Grant ran back to the window and crawled through. He made his way toward Daniel and Max, shouting their names and hearing their responses.

"Grant! I need your help!" Daniel was trying to pull Max out from underneath the large beam of wood that had fallen across his back. Max had laid down since Sarah was pulled to safety, but both ends of the beam were on fire, and it was quickly traveling towards Max. Grant reached them and grabbed Max's other arm, and the two pulled hard.

Even with both young men, they were unable to pull Max free. Grant yelled, "I have to try to get the beam off him!" He crawled around Max toward the beam. By this time, the fire had traveled to only inches from Max, and the only place for Grant to grab the board was already burning.

Without wasting another second, Grant took off his shirt and wrapped his hands.

"Grant!" shouted Max. "You two go! The eyewall is here!"

Grant didn't say a word. He grabbed the board and cried out loud as he pushed on the large beam. After a few seconds, Daniel took off his shirt and crawled over next to Grant. The two pushed and yelled together. They finally maneuvered the beam far enough for Max to crawl out.

After quickly shaking off their burning shirts, the Grant and Daniel helped Max to the window and lifted him through. Two men were waiting to help him to the ground. As Max was lowered, his shirt raised up and briefly exposed his midsection. The two men saw the large cut on his side Along with it were several scars across the lower part of his back. Grant quickly took off his shirt and applied pressure on the wound.

The wind was incredible! It must have been over 120 mph, and trees were snapping all around. There was nothing they could do but lie down and allow what was left of the house to block the wind. Fortunately, by this time the storm had brought enough rain to limit the fire's wrath.

Josh was trying to contact Stella at the camp with the hand radio, but was unsuccessful. He looked out the window of the truck toward the house just as half the roof tore off and disappeared into the night. "Max, where are you?" he thought. "I hope you're OK. God, take care of them—please."

Suddenly, something drew his attention. Something out of place was moving mysteriously off to the right of the burning house. Josh squinted his eyes to see. The rain was driving from right to left, and the wind was plowing through. But Josh definitely saw something—no, it was someone!

Suddenly, he gasped, and a look of horror filled his face. A man was stumbling toward them. He fell to his knees, and the wind caused him to roll many times. It was too difficult to see who it was, but he was wearing a white robe. Chris, with his eyes still closed, mumbled again, "Save Dad. Josh, we have to save Dad."

CHAPTER SIX

Saturday, September 24, 2005. 4:30 AM

"Max, come in. Max, can you hear me. This is Stella—Josh, Max—is anyone there?" Stella put the hand radio on the kitchen table next to a map showing the way to the Sonnier's house. She laid her head in her hands with her elbows resting on the table. It had been two hours since they left, and it crossed her mind to drive out there to find them.

The dining hall's big kitchen lit up when a couple walked in with a flashlight. Stella raised up and shined her flashlight in their direction; it was Rob and Christa Emanual. They noticed tears on Stella's face, and Christa hugged her tightly.

"Are the kids asleep?" Stella asked.

"Yes, they finally gave it up. Any word from Max?" Christa asked as she gently pulled away from hugging Stella.

"No. I'm terrified something has happened," said Stella as she began to weep.

"I'm sure they're OK. It looks like it's calming a bit outside. I think we're in the eye," comforted Christa.

Max had led Rob to faith in Christ soon after Christa's salvation, and the two men became solid friends over the weeks. Their wives had also formed a solid friendship over the few, short weeks together, and they knew this friendship would last a lifetime.

"Max is a smart man," said Rob. "He knows what to do to keep safe." Rob noticed the map on the table. He looked at Stella and asked, "Is that the map to the Sonnier's house? Give it to me; I'll go look for them."

Stella's eyes widened. "You will?" Just then static blared from the hand radio. Stella pressed the transmitter button, "Max! Are you there?" They listened for a response but only heard more bits of static.

"Maybe they're on their way back and just coming into range," encouraged Christa. They listened for a minute more but heard nothing. Stella was about to put the radio back on the table when she heard her husband's voice, "Stella, it's me."

Pulling into the camp wasn't as dangerous as leaving. They were in the eye of the hurricane. Josh maneuvered the truck as close to the dining hall as he could, and Max followed close behind in Chris' truck.

They quickly carried in Chris' family, who was beginning to wake up. Chris had a nasty bruise on his shoulder and a nice bump on the head, but he was alert enough to walk in on his own. He felt tremendous relief as his pregnant wife and son were lying restfully on a mattress inside a safe place surrounded by friends.

Just then, Chris looked up and saw a man standing before him. He was wearing a white robe and calling his name. "Chris. I am so sorry."

It was Chris' neighbor, Old Man John. Still in his pajamas and robe, John walked over to Chris and hugged him. "I am sorry for telling you to stay home."

"It wasn't your fault, Mr. John. I would've stayed anyway. I'm just so glad we're OK. I'm glad you're OK!" Chris gave the elderly man a gentle bear hug.

After Grant and Daniel were treated for their first degree burns on their hands and arms, they walked into the kitchen to find Max and Stella. One of the camp nurses was stitching his wound.

"Well, it looks like neither of you will be using your fists any time soon," joked Max. The two boys snickered. "Perhaps these two families might be friends after all."

"How's your back, Mr. McClain?" Daniel asked. "Can I see?"

Max paused. Then he raised his shirt to reveal the nurse's handiwork.

"It's gonna take at least fifty stitches, and he probably has a broken rib or two, but he'll be fine," the nurse said.

Grant moaned as he stepped to his right. Daniel quickly caught him before he landed unconscious on the floor.

"Hey! Grant! You OK?" asked Daniel. He helped him sit down to catch his breath.

Grant mumbled a bit. Then he said, "I don't do so well with blood."

Max spoke up, "But you did great with a hurricane and fire." Grant smiled.

"Boys," Max continued, "I'm very proud of you two. You showed bravery and great care for others, especially me. Thank you for saving my life." The two boys looked at each other. They each held up their hands and bumped fists.

It was now 11:30 a.m. on Saturday morning. Several children were still trying to sleep, but most of the people who had hunkered down in the dining hall were now venturing out to see the results of Rita's wrath. Max had never seen this many trees down. Buildings were cut in half by pines and oaks.

He could barely see the ground for all the limbs, broken roofing material, and insulation. Dozens of corrugated roofing tin were twisted up in several trees, but just as Max had figured, the dining hall withstood the storm with only slight damage. He gathered those who were outside into a group and led in a prayer of thanksgiving to God for their safety. There were tears of joy from most of the people gathered around.

Tuesday, September 27, 2005. 3:14 PM

Three days later, much of the debris was piled into various places. A few people showed up with chainsaws and were hard at work cleaning the grounds. The power was still out, so Charlie and his son, Rog, took charge in grilling the meat from the walk-in freezer as it thawed. And they made Branson, the thief, serve each family a large tray of food.

Each meal was like a backyard party with laughter, storm stories, and kids running and playing. The people from the surrounding area, many of them Christians, were bonding with the Katrina evacuees. They were trading their contact information, planning to stay in touch.

Several Christians from the town had shared their faith in Christ and invited the Katrina evacuees to their church. They even gave names to their two different groups: the Katrinas and the Ritas. These two culturally different groups had become virtually inseparable due to the commonality they now shared—a massive storm and its destruction.

Ritas were helping Katrinas, and Katrinas were working with Ritas remodeling their damaged homes. But on one particular day, Josh was missing.

Max turned the diesel truck into the dirt driveway that led to the burnt house. It was still smoldering, and the grounds around it were black with soot. A few of the surrounding trees had burned due to the high winds that carried the flames. In fact, the whole place looked like a bomb had exploded.

He spotted someone sitting on a pile of firewood that had been blown over. Josh was facing the once standing house. Max put the truck in park, killed the ignition, got out, and walked over to the pile of wood. He stepped up on a couple of logs and sat next to Josh.

After a minute of silence, Max spoke up, "Why don't you tell me what's on your mind?"

Josh took in a deep breath and exhaled slowly. "Yeah. Just needed to get away for a while. Need to clear my head."

"A clear head is good for the mind," replied Max. He picked up a small piece of wood and threw it toward the house.

"You know, I hated the Church when I was in high school," said Josh.

"Yeah, you've told me before."

"I had a lot of bitterness stored up for a long time. It would've killed me if you hadn't showed up." Josh glanced at Max and then back at the Sonnier's house. "It is good to see Chris again."

"Yes it is," replied Max. "Josh, what's troubling you?"

Josh paused for a while before answering. "I felt—I was bitter before Rita hit. So much opportunity to reach out to the Katrinas—but many of the church folks around here just came by to see what they could take from the supplies that weren't meant for them. I felt hatred rising in my gut, and a part of me justified it, even though I knew it was wrong."

"I understand. I was frustrated, too," said Max.

"But now things are different. Those same church people are here because of the same reason the Katrinas are. Now they are building relationships with them, and rightly using those relationships to show God's love."

"So why are you bothered by this?"

"I'm not—I'm not bothered by what I see now. But, Max, you saw all this. It took a storm the size of Rita to change the mindset of Christians around here." Josh hung his head low. It was obvious something was depressing him.

"Sometimes God uses something this drastic to get His people to do what He commanded us to do," responded Max. "We've been praying God would break our hearts for what breaks His."

Josh picked up his head. He had tears in his eyes as he looked at the burnt house. "But how long will it last, Max? How long will we keep this mindset?" He picked up a piece of wood and threw it toward the house.

"I almost lost my family in that fire. Besides Mom in Oklahoma, they're the only family I have. It took a storm to bring my brother and me back together, but how long will it last?" He looked at Max with anguish in his eyes. Max put his arm around Josh and pulled him into his once-bleeding side.

"I don't know. Let's talk to God about it."

Wednesday, September 28, 2005. 1:23 PM

A black Ford Crown Vic with tinted windows pulled through the camp's entrance to the front of the office. Both front doors opened and two men with suits and shades stepped out and walked toward the office door.

The driver asked his partner, "Did you check us in?"

"Yeah, I checked us in," he said with frustration.

"This micromanagement system sucks," said the driver.

Stella was startled at the knock on the front office door. During these last several weeks no one knocked. Everyone had become more like family members than campers. She got up from her office chair and opened the door. The two suits were standing there, seemingly waiting for Stella to make the first move.

"Hello, Sirs. Can I help you?" Stella was obviously confused at the visit of such well-suited men.

"My name is Agent Daniels. This is Agent Wright. We're with the FBI." The agent flipped open his wallet showing his ID. Stella gave a slight chuckle. This is right out of the movies, she thought to herself. "May we come in?" asked Agent Daniels.

"Sure. Come on in." She opened the door all the way, allowing the suits to walk through. Agent Wright slightly paused and gave her a noticeable look above his Ray Bans. Then he followed his partner into the office. "Can I offer you something to drink? Coffee? Iced water?"

"No, thank you," replied Daniels. Both men sat in the foyer's cushioned chairs.

"OK. So how can I help you? We're not quite used to having the FBI out here," said Stella.

"Ma'am, we have a few questions to ask you regarding some orphans from a village in Peru," asked Daniels.

"The children! Are they OK?"

"Yes, ma'am. The children are fine. Please sit down," ordered Wright.

Stella sat down, but asked, "Where are they? What's this about?"

"Please, Mrs. McClain, we have a few questions to ask."

"OK," replied Stella, "fine. At least take off your sun glasses." Both men gave each other a look, then turned back toward Stella and removed their shades.

"Mrs. McClain," began Daniels, "we need to know of your relationship with these children and the United Adoption Agency."

"Uh, well—there's really not much of one. My husband and I were planning to visit a couple of the families a few days ago who hosted some of the children, but the hurricane changed our plans."

"Why were you planning to visit them?" asked Wright.

Stella looked at him, almost spelling out idiot with her countenance. Realizing her rudeness, she straightened up and answered, "We want to adopt, and we found the United Adoption Agency as the best place for us to work with."

Daniels chimed in, "Can you tell us what you know of this place?"

"The UAA? Well, it has been around for many years—like, at least thirty—"

"Can you tell us about the leadership?" asked Wright.

Stella shrugged her shoulders. "What do you wanna know? They're great ladies with a great volunteer staff. Naomi Kris took over for her mom who had died a few years back."

"Do you know where most of the children come from?" Stella stopped with a frown. It was at that question that she became tired of answering and desired to know why they were really here.

"Why don't you tell me what's going on? Why is the FBI here asking me questions about the UAA and the Peruvian children?"

"Ma'am, we would like to speak with your husband. Could you get him for us?" requested Agent Daniels.

"Max? Why? What's going on?"

"Please, Mrs. McClain. Just go get your husband." Stella realized she wasn't going to get any answers out of the FBI. She stood up, excused herself, and left the building.

With an eighteen-inch Poulan chainsaw in his hands, Max was hard at work sawing the fallen trees into sections small enough to carry. Stella carefully walked behind him and tapped on his back. His shirt was soaked with sweat and covered with sawdust.

Max noticed his wife and turned off the chainsaw. Stella immediately started, "Max, you won't believe this, but the FBI is here, in our office, demanding to know information about Naomi and the children from Peru."

"What? Naomi Kris?" asked Max.

"They're asking to speak with you now. Max, we've been through this. I'm sure they want you back."

Max breathed in a deep sigh and sat the Poulan on the ground. "OK. Let's go."

"Why is the FBI here asking about Naomi?" asked Stella as they walked toward the office.

"We'll find out."

As they rounded the corner of the multipurpose building with the office in view, they noticed the black Ford Crown Vic speeding out of the camp. Max and Stella looked at each other and then picked up their pace.

Max entered first and darted toward his office. He stopped at the entrance. Stella peaked around from behind him. Every drawer of his desk was opened, papers were scattered everywhere, filing cabinet drawers were opened—the place looked like Hurricane Rita had returned.

"What in the world?" shouted Stella.

Max maneuvered his way to a filing cabinet. The lock had been broken. He flipped around a few manila folders, tossing some of them aside, and then stopped. Stella asked what he was doing, but he didn't answer. He just stood there with that look on his face that said Don't bother me—I'm thinking.

Stella spoke up, "Max, what's wrong? Why was the FBI here going through all your stuff?"

"Honey," Max said, looking at his bride, "everything will be OK. I'm sorry, but I need you to trust me."

Stella gazed deep into her lover's hazel green eyes. "I trust you." With that he turned around, stood in his desk chair and lifted a ceiling tile. He reached inside the ceiling, paused and looked at Stella, and then pulled out a well-sealed, legal-sized envelope.

He stepped down to the floor and handed the envelope to Stella. "I want you to give this to Josh. Tell him to hide it in a secure place and to tell no one where it is."

Stella took the envelope. Then one of the female volunteers walked in the office. "Oh wow! They did this?" she said.

"What do you mean they?" asked Max.

The volunteer answered, "Well, I walked into the office, and I saw these two men. They said they were with the FBI. They asked me if they could just have a look around. I didn't know what else to say."

"It's OK. You didn't do anything wrong," said Max. "Stella, you know what to do."

Friday, September 30, 2005

It was amazing! The friendships did not cease. The Katrinas were supposed to be relocated all over the country by government-delegated agencies, but the Christians of the area requested to accept full responsibility for finding homes for them in their own town.

It was one week since Rita hit, and skilled carpenters were hired to rebuild Camp Pinerock. Max went back outside and enjoyed seeing the demolition of the buildings that took damage from the storm. As each wall came down, his mind was flooded with a vast number of memories that took place in the buildings, and it brought a sense of nostalgia. However, he knew something wonderful was going to be built in their places.

What he enjoyed more was the inspiration he received from Josh. The talk they had on the pile of firewood at Chris Sonnier's house fueled a fire deep within Max that had become inextinguishable. Looking around at the people, he stood tall with a smile that caused creases at the outer corners of his eyes. And he felt the Spirit's leading him to do something quite different—something quite extraordinary.

After what he had seen God do these last several weeks, he knew God was definitely moving in this town. He wanted, above all, to be a part of it, but he also wanted to see the children from the United Adoption Agency.

Josh and Chris sat in the rocking chairs just outside the dining hall. They hadn't spent this much time together in quite a while. Small talk was the big topic of their conversation, and then both became quiet for a couple minutes until Chris spoke.

"Josh, thanks for coming. Thank you…for saving our lives," said Chris, staring off in the distance. Josh thought carefully before responding.

"You'd do the same for me. I'm just glad you're still here. I'm glad we're both here."

A couple minutes passed before Chris spoke up again. "I miss Dad."

"I know," said Josh. "I miss him, too." The only noise they could hear for another minute was the squeaking of their rocking chairs and the distant pounding of hammers.

"I was jealous of you, Josh. Ever since you were adopted, I looked at you as competition for Mom and Dad's affection and attention."

Josh sat and rocked quietly. He had prayed for this moment to happen for a long time. And he prayed now that he and his brother would be fully reconciled.

Chris continued, still looking off in the distance, "It was unfair to you. I am sorry for the way I treated you. You're my brother, and—and I love you." Chris wiped his eyes. He blinked and turned away so Chris wouldn't notice. They hadn't spoken to one another in three years.

Finally, because of a storm and a fire, the two men were brothers. Reconciliation reigned.

Saturday, October 1, 2005. 10:23 AM

The Camp sent word to all the pastors and church leaders to join Max McClain in a key meeting related to the consequences of the two storms. Ladies from each church supplied lunch for the meeting. The turnout was more than Max had expected.

In the past, pastors' luncheons sponsored by the camp brought in about a dozen people, but this meeting packed the conference room with over fifty! It was clear God's Spirit was moving mightily, and Max wanted to be sensitive to His leading.

After lunch, Max stood and looked over the many pastors and leaders from the surrounding communities. Several of them had heard of the events that had taken place during the storm, of the fire, and how Max and his crew had worked tirelessly and sacrificially to care for the Katrinas and Ritas.

They saw, first hand, what "sacrificing for the Kingdom" looked like. They knew his philosophy of ministry: Do what it takes to reach people for Christ—even if it means sacrificing your own life. And now they had come to listen to a man of God whom they had seen practice what they had been preaching for many years.

Max thanked everyone for coming and the ladies for providing the wonderful meal. Then he opened his Bible.

"Matthew 5:13-16. You are the salt of the earth. But if the salt loses its saltiness, how can it be made salty again? It is no longer good for anything, except to be thrown out and trampled by men. You are the light of the world. A city on a hill cannot be hidden. Neither do people light a lamp and put it under a bowl. Instead they put it on its stand, and it gives light to everyone in the house. In the same way, let your light shine before men, that they may see your good deeds and praise your Father in heaven.

"James 2:14-17. What good is it, my brothers, if a man claims to have faith but has no deeds? Can such faith save him? Suppose a brother or sister is without clothes and daily food. If one of you says to him, 'Go, I wish you well; keep warm and well fed,' but does nothing about his physical needs, what good is it? In the same way, faith by itself, if it is not accompanied by action, is dead.

"Matthew 9:35-38. Jesus went through all the towns and villages, teaching in their synagogues, preaching the good news of the kingdom and healing every disease and sickness. When he saw the crowds, he had compassion on them, because they were harassed and helpless, like sheep without a shepherd. Then he said to his disciples, 'The harvest is plentiful but the workers are few. Ask the Lord of the harvest, therefore, to send out workers into his harvest field.'"

Max looked up. They were all on the edge of their seats. He continued, "I have read those passages many, many times over the years, and, I'm sure, you have preached through them. But they have never become as alive in my heart as they are now."

Placing his Bible on the table he continued, "I have never been more tired than I am now. Never been more spent. Never been more—" As he looked at his wife, her beauty shined in her gentle smile at him, and he finished his sentence with a bright smile in return, "joyful."

"When Katrina hit," he continued, "all I could think was how we could help. I thought about encouraging all of us to take up a love offering and send money. Perhaps we could send canned food, or bottles of water, or something we thought they needed. I thought about putting together a team to go to New Orleans to help.

"I never, in a million years, would have thought about scrapping two months of planned camping retreats in order to host hundreds of evacuees—some of which who would seem quite unthankful for our hospitality. I already had my ministry planned for God's Kingdom, and it was justified by our own measure of success.

"It's time to be honest and open. Many of us in this room have been salt that was only good for the trampling of men." No one moved a muscle when he said that. He continued, "We have been lanterns that only light up inside the four walls we call 'church.' As churches in this town, our severe lack of Christian deeds has rendered our faith useless—dead. And before Rita hit, when the multitudes of needy people were here, most of us came by the camp with compassion only for our own selfish desires rather than for the people and their desperate need of a loving Savior."

Most of the men stared at the floor. A few others looked at each other, but quickly turned their gaze to something else.

Max continued, "Most of us in this very room have been living for the kingdom we have built on this earth, instead of the Kingdom Jesus is building in heaven—our celestial, eternal home." He paused and looked around the room at each of their faces. Then he continued with a calming voice.

"But that was before a destructive storm hit us. Since then, I have witnessed things that Jesus, Himself, did while on earth. I have seen our Christian people love those who were difficult to love. We have given ourselves to those who are far less fortunate. We have opened our homes to those who are homeless. And we have spoken words of the gospel that match the love we have shown.

"To borrow from a friend of mine, we have found our radius. We have begun to look outside our windows to see those who are hungry and naked, and we have forsaken our comfort to feed and clothe them. We have sacrificed to provide, and Christ is honored because of our obedience to His command to let our lights shine before men."

There is a certain kind of smile that only powerful inspiration brings, and this smile formed on all the faces in the room. A few of the men wiped their eyes as they listened to Max.

With increasing passion and intensity Max continued, "We are a different town now! We are unlike what we were before the storm, but it took this storm to transform us into what we are today—right now. God changed us, and each of us in this room, I am convinced, would never wish for our town to go back to what we were." He paused again—for several seconds of silence. Then he concluded with a simple question, "Or am I wrong?"

Max stopped. He looked around the room into each of their eyes. They began to look around, too, as if looking for someone who was supposed to answer out loud.

Finally an elderly man stood to his feet and pounded the table before him as he shouted, "We must never go back! Never, ever go back!"

Everyone turned to see the pastor who spoke with such passion. "I've seen the people in our church do things these last few weeks that have made me proud as their founding pastor. They have sacrificed to meet the needs of the Katrinas. And they have inspired me to do the same."

Another man stood up, "He's right! It took a storm to change us! We can never revert back to what we were. I'll be open and honest with you. Several of us have been competing with one another for church growth so we can have the numbers we want on Sunday morning."

The man's voice began to quiver, "I have been competing. I have been jealous. In fact, my own church turned down an opportunity to house some evacuees just so we can have the room to have our own services. But after what's been going on these last few weeks, I realize it's not about how we can just fill up our auditoriums with bodies on Sunday mornings."

Soon, many were voicing their agreements, and it went on for a couple minutes until Max brought them back to order.

"So we represent different local churches in our town and surrounding communities. We may differ on a few things, but we all stand on the truth that Christ died for our sins and rose from the dead, that no one can save himself from his own sin, but that he must trust in Christ alone to save. Now time for us to work—the Body of Christ in this town—purposed to deliver His gospel to our surroundings and disciple them to do the same.

"There's a large circle around us, and within that circle are neighborhoods, schools, businesses—people! In many ways, the whole world is our circle. It is time we work together to follow in obedience to Christ's command to spread His love in deed and in word.

"We're doing it now! Why stop? Why live like we were? Why not live life above the common, ordinary way of the world? That's what Christ has given us: life meant to live above the common."

It was silent in the room. Something was happening. There was a flurry in Max's gut, and a presence in the air. He silently prayed, "God, please move in our hearts!" He desperately wanted Christ to be honored by a unanimous desire to obey Him.

Someone spoke from the corner of the room. It was a soft, calming voice, and it was a simple prayer.

"Dear Father, I confess to You that I have been leading Your church to ask the question, 'What will it take for us to pack out our building on Sunday mornings?' Instead, help me to lead Your people to ask, 'What will it take for us to reach the nations with the gospel?'"

It was quiet for about two minutes. Sobbing could be heard. Sniffing and weeping were scattered throughout the room. That prayer led to many others making confession to God for leading the churches to be something different than what God commanded them to be.

Some confessed the sin of worshipping entertainment. Others confessed the sin of watering down the gospel. And one pastor confessed the sin of not using Scripture at all.

Two hours of praying and worshipping together passed—praying for one another, praying for more laborers, and thanking God for humbling them.

Then one of the pastors shared an idea. "Max, this radius thing you mentioned a while ago; it makes a lot of sense to me. I'd like to formally commit to you all that I will do what it takes to inspire our church to put our faith to action. What if we made a formal commitment to one another? What if we held each other accountable for this?"

"I'll make that commitment. Where do I sign?" said another.

The excitement was overwhelming! Max was on cloud nine and could hardly believe what was going on. He hoped it was more than just emotion, but a real, gut-level, God-led commitment from the people in the conference room.

"Listen. We have carpenters outside who are rebuilding our camp," Max said. "They are trained people who know how to effectively build sturdy facilities, and they do this all the time. If we are going to stick with our commitment, we need to be well trained. I think we haven't been going outside our church buildings because we don't know how. We need to invest our time, money, and energy in getting trained to effectively bring the gospel to people.

"In fact," he continued, "I'd like for us to think about focusing on reaching children. My heart is tearing inside right now because of some Peruvian orphans who are here in America waiting to be adopted. My wife and I are planning to adopt one of them. Maybe more. We haven't heard from them since the hurricane. Reaching children—something inside is calling me to reach children.

"I've read statistics that 85% of believers today trusted in Christ before their 18th birthday. Here is a great opportunity—if we could be as passionate about reaching children as we have become about reaching evacuees during a hurricane, then we could change the next generation by sharing the love of Jesus Christ to children today."

It was a specific vision—a mission of dedication, perseverance, and determination. A unanimous decision was made to form an alliance purposed to inspire their churches to become well trained to reach children and their families with the gospel, both in word and in deed.

Tuesday, October 4, 2005

They called it The RADIUS Initiative.

It was officially formed by the local churches, the camp, and several Christian-owned businesses. Its purpose was to inspire Christians to become passionate to bring the gospel to their own circles and beyond. Prayer and training were essential to being effective. Their next step was to seek an organization that was successful in training believers to reach children for Christ.

It was lunch time at the camp. Several were in the dining hall enjoying their meal and fellowship. Max and Stella were at a table with Rob and Christa and their kids when Max's cell phone rang.

"Max McClain," he answered. He stared into the distance as he listened. Stella slowly put her fork down on her plate and kept her gaze on her husband. She could tell this was an unusual phone call. "Stay put, Rachel. We're on our way."

CHAPTER SEVEN

"What's going on?" asked Stella.

"Come with me," he replied.

"It's time I fill you in," Max began while driving down the curvy, backwoods road. "A little over a month ago I received an envelope in the mail from Naomi Kris. Inside was a list of the families who hosted the children from Peru."

"A list of the families? Why would she send you that?" interrupted Stella.

"I'm getting there. She had a small note inside the envelope that instructed me to keep them in a safe place. She said I was the only one she could trust. So I called her to find out more." Max paused.

"And?"

"She said that something unusual was going on with the kids. Nothing bad—just unusual. For instance, one little girl had fallen hard on her knee, but there was no scrape—no mark at all. The girl wasn't even crying. There was no pain.

"Another little boy was hit in the face with a baseball, but nothing showed up—no swelling or bruising. She said things like this seemed to have been happening often. Kids would play, but never get hurt. Accidents would happen as with all kids, but no injuries would occur."

"OK, I admit. That sounds a little odd. But why send you the list of their families?"

"One night Naomi received a call from someone claiming to be from the FBI. He was asking a lot of questions about the children. Weird questions—like, how often does she administer medicine, or take the kids to the doctor, or things like that. She thought the conversation was very strange. She said his name was Agent Daniels. I remember a Daniels—shady guy."

"That is strange. One of the agents who came to the camp called himself Daniels," said Stella.

"The next day, she said she called the FBI back, but she couldn't get any information. Then a couple of men from the FBI came to her office asking about the list of the families and their contact information. She tried to avoid the conversation at first, but they kept pushing. She finally gave them a fake list and then mailed the original to me. Then she deleted it from her computer."

"Why didn't she just call the police?"

"I don't know. She was probably scared. These men claimed to be with the FBI."

"Do you think they are for real?"

"Darlin', from what I've seen in the past, anything's possible. It wouldn't be the first time," answered Max.

Stella sat and stared at Max for a few seconds. Then she spoke, "Why didn't you tell me all this?"

"I'm sorry. This is not your run-of-the-mill camp drama. Something dangerous is going on. I didn't want you in the middle of it."

"So who was just on the phone?" asked Stella.

"That was Rachel Willard. She's with the children at the hospital in Lake Charles."

"Hospital? What happened?"

"The children are OK," replied Max. He shook his head, squinted his eyes, and continued, "And that's just it."

Stella glared at Max, trying to figure out what he meant. "What happened, Max?"

"They were apparently heading to Houston for shelter before the storm hit, but the bus wrecked—flipped on its side. The driver didn't make it."

Stella put her hand over her mouth—she couldn't breathe for a moment. He continued, "Naomi is stable, but in critical condition. Rachel was banged up a bit, but she's OK. The children—all, but one, are perfect."

Max turned toward Stella and concluded, "Not a single scratch. Rachel is pretty scared something is about to happen with the children."

Stella noticed Max tilt his head. He was noticeably confused at something. "What's wrong, Max? What is it?"

Max breathed in deeply. "It's this Agent Daniels. I was always suspicious of him. Something just wasn't right about him."

Mike Sage pulled his car into his usual parking spot at his church office. As he entered the double glass doors, he noticed Rick Nash sitting in the office foyer reading a magazine from the stack on the coffee table next to him.

Rick was a new pastor from Illinois. He took the Methodist church in town about a year ago, and the two had met for lunch several times to get to know each other.

Rick was a tall, slender fellow with a gentle demeanor. Mike's outgoing personality was a welcome to Rick, and Mike enjoyed his new friendship, as well.

"Hey, there, Rick. What's going on with you today?" asked Mike.

"Hey," replied Rick standing and shaking hands with his friend. "Just wanted to come by and bounce something off ya, if you have a few."

"Sure, come on in." They entered Mike's office. Rick sat as Mike poured the two a cup of coffee. Then he joined him in the nearby chair. "What's up, my friend?"

"This Radius Initiative. I have a thought."

Mike took a sip of his coffee and said, "This is pretty exciting to see what's going on in our town, isn't it? I have never been to quite a meeting of pastors as we had at the camp the other day. What's your idea?"

"When I was in Illinois, our church partnered with an organization that specialized in reaching children with the gospel. It was inexpensive, but the training was top-notch.

"They trained us and set us up with an elementary public school. That first year, Mike, we shared the gospel with 60 kids in that one school. Half of them trusted in Christ, and several of them and their families joined our church. The next year we added an apartment ministry through this organization.

"Today, that church reaches out to about 400 families. Their church has grown by conversion. It has been amazing, Mike. Just amazing!"

Mike put his coffee down. "Wow. Growth by conversion—now that's a novel idea."

"Exactly. And I'm thinking to myself, Why don't we do this here? I mean, our Radius Initiative has really inspired us to do something above the common, ordinary way of doing church, right?"

"Children. Max is right. This is exactly what we need. You know, Rick, I read recently that it's unfortunate we sometimes view the children's ministry as a babysitting program, but that we can actually change the culture of our society in the next generation by impacting children for Christ today. I like this idea. Who is this organization? Do you think they would help us here?"

"They call themselves the Child Evangelism Fellowship," replied Rick. Then he sipped his coffee.

"Hi, I am Agent Daniels with the FBI. I'd like to ask you a couple of questions." The suit flipped open his wallet revealing an ID to the doctor on call.

"Sure, how can I help?" replied the doctor.

"First of all, what is the condition of the group of children that were brought in recently?" The agent asked as he stuffed his wallet into his hip pocket.

The doctor, who had been given strict orders not to divulge any information to anyone, looked around. He was clearly uncomfortable with answering any questions regarding the amazing children, but this was the FBI. How could he refuse the government?

"Well, uh, they're doing well," answered the doctor.

"That's great. Listen, I need to interview a few of these children. Would you show me where they are?"

"I'd really like to know why the FBI is involved. This is just a traffic accident. Don't the police usually handle this?" asked the doctor.

The agent removed his Ray Bans as an attempt to intimidate. "Doctor—" He leaned in to see the doctor's name tag on his white coat. "Reynolds, I am a special agent with the Federal Bureau of Investigation. I am investigating a mystery involving these children. You don't want to hinder my investigation. Please take me to the children."

The doctor didn't hesitate to reply, "That's fine, and all. But you need to understand that we've been working tirelessly around the clock for several days now. I am exhausted. And I want to know what's going on with these kids."

Max drove the car onto the third level of the parking garage of Lake Charles Memorial Hospital. When they walked through the double doors Rachel ran toward them and embraced Stella. Her eyes were bloodshot, her hair unkept, and she seemed quite delusional.

"I'm so glad you are here! The last few days have been horrible."

"How are you? How is Naomi?" asked Stella.

"She's hurt, but she'll be OK. Mr. McClain, four of the children are missing! We can't find them anywhere! They're missing!" Rachel was getting more hysterical by the second.

Just then, Max caught the sound of loud voices coming from down the hall. He turned to see a man in a black suit arguing with a doctor.

Rachel squinted her tired eyes to see the agent and the doctor who were about 30 yards away. Then her eyes lit up as the memory came to her,

"Hey, that's one of the men who came to our office last month! Mr. McClain, that's him! That's the one Naomi told you about!"

The agent heard Rachel's desperate voice and looked toward them.

"Max, that's Agent Daniels who was at the camp," explained Stella.

"Yeah, I know him," said Max. "You two stay here. I wanna have words with this so-called FBI agent."

Max began walking toward Agent Daniels, but Stella protested, "Max, wait."

Suddenly, the suit threw on his shades and took off in the opposite direction. Max immediately shouted to the nearest nurse, "Call security! Tell them to lock down the hospital!" With that he dashed after Daniels.

Max chased the agent down the hall and around a corner. The agent sprinted toward an empty elevator that was closing its doors. Max sped up—trying to catch the doors before they closed, but he didn't make it.

Max quickly noticed the elevator going up, so he ran around the corner to the stairwell. Skipping every other stair, he made his way to the parking garage and heard the elevator's bell ding. He ran to the doors just as they were opening.

He stopped. He had no expression on his face as he began to back up slowly. Out of the elevator, the suited man carefully walked toward Max. He was pointing a .40 caliber semi-automatic pistol at Max's forehead.

"Don't move." A voice came from behind. Someone grabbed both his hands and bound them with a large zip tie. Max turned to see the other suit with a 9mm pistol pointed at him. Agent Daniels reached into his inside coat pocket and retrieved his cell phone. He dialed and held the phone to his ear.

"Sir," said Daniels, "we have McClain. What do you want us to do?"

Daniels listened for a few seconds, and then placed his cell back in his pocket. Wright spoke up, "What did he say?"

"He said to bring him in."

With that, the two suits led Max to their Crown Victoria and threw him into the back seat. Agent Wright got in the back with him, and Daniels got into the driver's seat, started the car, and sped off.

Clif Tyler had just hung up the phone when his secretary informed him of another call. "This is Clif, how can I help you?"

"Hi Clif, my name is Mike Sage, pastor at First Baptist of Caroline Springs. Do you have a few minutes?"

"Sure, go ahead, Mike."

Mike filled Clif in on the whole story of the storm at Camp Pinerock, the Katrina's and Rita's, and the Radius Initiative. He shared the passion of the churches to reach out to the community, especially to the children, and asked for help.

Clif was astonished at the work of the Lord around Caroline Springs. He shared words of wisdom to Mike and assured him that Child Evangelism Fellowship would be there to aid in reaching children for Christ.

"Mike, I'm going to put you in touch with one of our Senior Ministry Coordinators. Let's see, that would be Dale Jackson," replied Clif. "We can come to your church and begin setting up several ministries in your area in a matter of just a few weeks."

"What would this entail?" asked Mike.

"Well, we believe in the evangelism ministry coming from the local church. So, in 3 simple phrases: we inspire, train, and send off. Dale will provide great training to your volunteers, establish partnerships between churches and schools and apartment complexes, help get Good News Clubs started, and send you guys on your way. We're here for support, guidance—pretty much whatever help you may need in the future. We have all the material and training you need to reach those kiddos."

Mike's eyes widened as he was on the edge of his seat. "Wow! OK, so what are Good News Clubs?"

"You're gonna love this, Mike. We can actually get into the public school system. Good News Clubs are weekly after school programs provided by the church. It usually lasts around an hour, and it consists of Bible stories, games, snacks, songs, missionary stories, and the gospel is shared clearly each time. We've seen several thousand children saved each year across Louisiana through these events. They're incredible."

"This is exactly what we're looking for, Clif," said Mike.

"We also train teens to conduct 5-Day Clubs. This is kind of like VBS, but we go to the kids' turf. And the teens lead it."

"This is great. You have my contact info. Put me in touch with Dale—I look forward to the call. Thanks so much."

"You bet, Mike. God bless."

Mike sat back in his office chair and fantasized about his church reaching families in the community. He knew there were families who struggled with finding jobs and had financial strains. He realized there were children who were neglected and abused. He'd read the reports in the newspaper about sex trafficking women and children. This was their chance to bring the gospel to these children and their families and get them into their churches to nurture them.

He picked up a framed picture from his desk. It was his oldest daughter and her 2-year-old son. Mike's eyes watered. The little boy in the picture, his grandson, had no hair and had wires attached to his side just beneath his right arm. He spent the last year researching hundreds of alternative methods of treatment.

It was at that time he realized something powerful was working in his own heart. He would do anything to save the life of his grandson with neuroblastoma. And he would do anything to bring the salvation message to children throughout their community and beyond. This message of salvation brought the spiritual healing that only Christ can offer.

Mike prayed for months for God's passion for the salvation of children to be their's. What he needed was the endearing face of a child to be seared in his mind in order to gain that passion. Now he had it; it was the face of his grandson. Nothing would stop him from this mission with Child Evangelism Fellowship.

Security guards at the hospital were convening at the entrances of the facility, but Max had already been taken. Stella was sitting down weeping over the ordeal as Rachel stood rubbing her shoulders.

"Ma'am, I'm Officer Hendricks. Can I ask you a couple of questions?"

Stella looked up revealing her swollen, bloodshot eyes. "Yes, go ahead," she replied.

The officer squatted to be eye level with Stella. "Did you see who took your husband?"

Stella burst out her answer, "He was pretending to be FBI. Said his name was Agent Daniels. He and another were at our camp recently asking about the orphans that are here for a few weeks from Peru, but I don't know why they would take Max!"

"Why did they want info on these kids?" asked the officer.

"I'm not quite sure, but I think it has something to do with the children not being harmed in the bus crash."

"Can you tell me about this crash?"

"Well, all I know is that the bus driver, apparently, tried to avoid a car that swerved into his lane, and the bus flipped over. But none of the children were hurt. Well, just one, actually. But the bus driver was killed."

The officer stood up, finished jotting down notes in his tablet, and thanked Stella for her help. Stella stopped him before he walked away and asked, "Sir, what about the 4 missing children?"

"We're doing our best, ma'am."

It was quiet in the car for the first thirty minutes. Max sat in the back with his hands zip-tied behind him. He carefully twisted and pulled the plastic zip-tie—trying to get them loose enough for him to slip his hands through.

Finally, Agent Wright spoke up, "Mr. McClain, you need to tell us where the contact list is. You do this, and we will let you go."

"And if I don't?" responded Max in a calm voice.

"Mr. McClain," chimed in Daniels, "just tell us where the list is."

"What do you want with those kids?" asked Max.

The two suits ignored his questions and looked forward.

"So I take it you're playing both sides—FBI agents who are being paid off by someone to do their dirty work. That's my guess."

Daniels, ignoring Max, commented to his associate, "Uh-oh, we're almost on empty. You got any cash?"

"Are you kiddin'? They only give us sixty bucks a week for gas. I've got, like, fifteen left!"

Max continued. "I know you, Daniels. I always figured you to be a traitor to your country. So what do you expect to get out of me? You think you can pull information from me? You think you're that good?" Daniels ignored him.

Max knew torture. His 15 years as an FBI special agent led him down some dark roads. Would these two young men do the same?

"So where are you taking me? Beaumont? I've got lots of friends there. Someone will recognize me."

"No, we're not going to Beaumont, and no one will recognize you where we're going. It's way too big a place for you, so why don't you just sit back and relax 'til we get there." Wright's irritation was just what Max was aiming for.

Max reached into his back pocket and pulled out his cell phone. Without the ability to look, he felt the buttons by memory and activated the "text" feature. He hoped he was clear enough as he typed only one word, then he pressed the "send" button which sent the text to the last person he'd sent to before—Stella.

When he slid the phone back into his pocket, he prayed, "God, I don't know why You are allowing this to happen, but I trust You. I know you have this under control. Just give me wisdom—show me what to do."

"Josh, where are you?" Stella was nearly yelling in her phone when Josh answered.

"Hey, I'm with Chris. We're at his place trying to salvage a few things. What's wrong?"

"Josh, Max was just kidnapped. It was one of those fake FBI agents who came to the camp. I'm at the Memorial Hospital. Can you come get me?"

"Kidnapped? Did you call the police?" asked Josh.

"Yes. They're here working on it now. Please just come get me."

"OK. What about the children? Are they safe?"

"For now, yes. Just hurry, Josh." Stella pressed "end" on her phone and stuffed it in her hip pocket. But she didn't notice its vibration as she did so.

Josh immediately filled Chris in on the situation, and the two jumped in his truck and sped off toward Lake Charles.

After about an hour and a half, the black Crown Vic pulled into a parking lot. Max noticed a sign that read BioTech Worldwide, Inc. Houston Branch Office. Agent Daniels parked the car, and Wright helped Max out of the back seat.

With an agent on either side, Max was escorted to the back of the large, brick building. Daniels pulled out a scan card from his inside coat pocket and waved it in front of a computer box mounted on the wall next to the door.

As he did so, Max observed a line underneath the collar of Daniels' shirt. With a beep and a click, Wright opened the door and the three men walked through.

The hall was long and dark. There were few lights which made the place cold and dark. Max wondered what kind of company "BioTech" was, and what kinds of things they did.

The men heard a door shut from another hall to their left, and Max took the advantage of the distraction. He shoved Daniels hard against the wall on his right, and then head-butted Wright square in the head. Wright was out cold. He gave a powerful back kick to Daniels' torso, followed by a knee to his temple. Both men lay unconscious.

He quickly sat down on the floor with his hands underneath his knees. He picked up his feet and brought his hands in front. Then he jumped up and ran down the hall. He turned a corner to his left and then another to his right. He heard voices ahead, so he turned around. There was a door with a sign that read MAIN LAB. He turned the knob and bolted through.

A tall man with a white lab coat stood in the room with his back facing Max. Max tried to leave before the man turned around, but it was locked. Slowly, the scientist turned and faced him.

"Hello," greeted the scientist in a Russian accent. "You must be Mr. McClain. My name is Afon Sokolov."

Max tried the knob again, but he couldn't open the door. The man continued, "Now, now, Mr. McClain. You can't exit this way. So you might as well have a seat, and you and I can get to know each other a bit, hmm?" Max didn't move, so Afon asked again, "Please, have a seat."

Max needed information, especially about the missing children. So he sat and asked, "I know who you are, Afon. What do you want?"

The Russian smiled and then pulled up a chair and sat down directly across from Max. "You know," responded the man in slightly broken English, "my father has been working on experiment for over fifteen years. He almost get to the finishing point, and what happens? One man stands in the way."

Max stared into the man's eyes as he spoke, reading every facial expression. Afon continued, "One man…with apparent death wish. He hinders our progress and keep from success."

The Russian leaned in close to Max and continued, "Let me tell you something, Mr. McClain. My father is very, very obsessed with success. You will deliver to me this list I want."

"Why does Vladimir need these children?" asked Max.

"Why does Vladimir need these children," repeated Afon, sitting back in his chair. "OK. I will answer. He need these children because it is his job. He get to create masterpiece." The Russian raised up his arms eloquently with that statement, as if he considered his father to be some kind of artist.

"What kind of masterpiece?" asked Max.

"Oh, masterpiece that spell victory for a country. An end to all wars. Peace for Mother Russia. You like peace, Mr. McClain?"

"Not at the cost of innocent lives," replied Max.

"I never said he would kill the children."

"Right. So who pays you? Who does your father work for?"

"Let's just say he have job security—that his employer knows of war very well."

"And who would that be? Iran? Pakistan?" Afon smiled but did not answer. Max continued, "Did you kidnap some of these children?"

"Well, yes. Of course. My father need them for his work. But he need the others, too. That is why we need you."

Max was annoyed at the Russian being so straight forward, although he was glad to know who took them. Afon continued, "Don't worry. They are safe—well fed and well taken care of."

Max stood up and began to walk toward Afon, "You will tell me where these children are. Or I will find them, even if I have to tear every inch of this place apart."

Afon saw the fierceness in Max's eyes. "You have wife, yes?" he asked.

Suddenly, the fierceness in Max's eyes turned deadly. To threaten him was one thing, but to threaten Stella was unthinkable.

"You lay one hand on her, and I will—" Suddenly, the Russian pulled out a small, black handgun and fired directly toward Max. A dart stuck in the upper left portion of his chest. His vision immediately grew dim. He looked at Afon who tilted his head and squinted his eyes, watching Max drop to his knees.

He fell to the floor. Afon stood up, pulled out a set of keys from his coat pocket, and opened the door. He turned to look once more at Max, and then exited the room.

Josh and his brother raced into the hospital's main entry where Stella and Rachel were waiting. The two ladies jumped from their seats and rushed to meet them.

"Stella!" said Josh. Then he noticed Rachel. "Who's this?"

"Josh, this is Rachel Willard. She's the assistant director at UAA in New Orleans."

"Hello. Hi." Josh said smiling to Rachel.

"Josh! Focus," interrupted Stella. "Has Max tried to contact you?"

"No. He hasn't. Have you tried to call him?"

"Of course I have," she said as she quickly took out her phone. Then she noticed the text.

"It's from Max!" she shouted. She opened the text to read it.

"What does it say?" asked Chris.

"Hoiston," replied Stella. Then she spelled it, "H-o-i-s-t-o-n."

"Hoiston. What is that?" asked Josh.

"I don't know. If he's kidnapped, then how could he text?" said Stella.

"Maybe it's misspelled?" chimed in Rachel. All three looked right at her. "Well, maybe," she defended.

Josh thought to himself, What is this similar to? What does it look like?

"Houston!" he shouted. "They're taking him to Houston! Stella, go tell the police what we've found, and tell them to guard the children!" He and Chris immediately ran back to his truck and sped off.

Isabella seemed peaceful. Hooked up to a dozen wires and tubes, she laid in the hospital bed still in a coma. Her best friend, nine-year-old Kristina, loyally rejected any pressure to leave her friend's side. Kristina was the voice of Isabella. She spoke for her friend, and they were inseparable.

Standing at the door entry of Isabella's room, a doctor and nurse conversed.

"Why would one child suffer so much when all the others are perfectly unharmed?" asked the nurse.

The doctor shook his head, "It's beyond me. In fact, we're all baffled by this." The doctor noticed a news reporter and camera man enter the hallway. "Hey! No media!" he shouted. Then he pointed to two security officers, "You two, I said to keep the news people out!"

The nurse walked into the room and placed her hand on Kristina's shoulder. "Kristina, are you hungry?" she asked in Spanish.

Kristina looked at the nurse, and then back toward her friend lying in the bed. She replied in her language, "No, I won't eat until Isabella does."

"Honey," replied the nurse, "Isabella might sleep for a few days. Her body needs to rest. I think she would want you to get something to eat. You really need to."

"Well, OK," agreed Kristina. The nurse put her arm around Kristina and led her out of the room.

CHAPTER EIGHT

Dale Jackson walked into the Caroline Springs Café, looked around, and noticed two men sitting near the front window. They both wore khaki pants, brown shoes, and blazers.

"Hi there, Gentlemen, I'm Dale."

The two men looked up, and then to each other. They seemed a bit confused. Dale intervened, "Ah, let me guess. You were expecting a man."

"My apologies, Mrs. Jackson," said Mike. He stood and extended his hand for a shake. "My name is Mike Sage, pastor at First Baptist of Caroline Springs. This is my friend Rick Nash. He's at Pinemont United Methodist Church."

"No apologies necessary, Pastor Sage," said Dale, heartily shaking Mike's hand. She gave Rick a hand shake and then took her seat. "I am so thrilled to hear about your passion for reaching children with the gospel."

Rick replied, "Oh, it's not just us, Dale. There are at least 40 pastors included. They're from all over the parish."

Dale was stunned. She brushed her hair away from her face and asked, "Could you repeat that, please?"

Dr. Sokolov answered his cell as he walked into his office, "Da."

He listened as the voice on the line spoke in English, "This has gone too far. You've kidnapped him? What are you thinking?"

"Let me do my job, and you will be paid more than your annual wage," said the Russian.

"Listen, Dr. Sokolov, I've been doing a lot of thinking. My wife and I—we don't want to have a part in this anymore. You don't have to pay us anything. I've done what you've asked me to."

"Ah. I see. Well, I am sorry, but you cannot back out now. What's done is done. Trust me. My friends in Libya do not want to lose this opportunity, and they will do whatever it takes to take the advantage. So, you see, my friend, you do not want to back out now. Follow through with us. You will enjoy your reward immensely." With that, he ended the call.

His vision was blurry. It could have been minutes or hours, he had no idea, but Max woke with a splitting headache. Lying on the floor, he reached to his chest to feel where the dart had punctured him. It was gone. Then he realized his hands were free from the zip tie.

Not knowing how much time he would have, he quickly began searching for any kind of evidence to shed light on what kind of place BioTech Worldwide was. He found a desk and opened every drawer, thumbing through files and papers but found nothing that looked suspicious.

He ran over to a filing cabinet and jerked on the upper drawer. It was locked. He grabbed a nearby pair of scissors and jammed it in the lock—prying the drawer open. He flipped through several files. One read Kiruna, Sweden. Another read Vittangi. These names were familiar to him.

He pulled and opened the file. His eyes caught the words village, 800 inhabitants, CIP, no known cure.

There were many other files with medical terminology he didn't understand, but something else caught his eye. One file read CONGENITAL ANALGESIA. His curiosity led him to read through the documents. He closed the folder and stuffed it under his arm.

Max flipped through more files and finally came upon names of people. David and Natalie Homestead. Fredrick and Rosanne Lockwood. John and Kristine Rabinski. None of these were familiar, and the first two names had the word rejected highlighted afterwards. He pulled the Rabinski file and read the words eligible for adoption, sum $100,000, and Occobamba.

It was the word adoption that caused him to gasp, but when he saw the name on the next file, his heart jumped. He pulled the file and stared at it. His face grew pale. He became nauseated. He was afraid to open it—surely this is a mistake. Surely this was a coincidence!

He heard distant voices down the hall. He grabbed the files he needed and rushed to another door in the lab. He quietly opened it and walked through—closing the door quietly behind him. This was the experimental part of the lab—there were beacons and burners, computers and scanners, microscopes and all kinds of various scientific-looking equipment everywhere.

Max walked around, keeping mind of the voices he heard down the hall. He saw a white lab coat hanging on the wall and grabbed it. Then he came to a large case of shelves with glass containers. Each container had labels with medical jargon typed on it.

He walked through another door when he heard the sounds of patter and scratching. There were at least 2 dozen cages of rats. Some seemed lethargic while others were quite active.

Max leaned in to see one of the calmer rats. Suddenly, the rat jumped at the wall of the cage, right at Max's head. He jumped back, and then smiled—laughing at himself under his breath.

He looked more closely at the rat—much of the hair on around its face had fallen out, and its skin appeared to be scaling.

As he was backing up, the door behind him burst open. Max turned around quickly to see a young man in a white coat standing in front of him. The scientist frowned and asked, "Who are you? What are you doing in here?"

He straightened up and answered, "Hi, there. I'm Doctor...Jones. Henry Jones. I'm the new guy." Max forced a smile as he extended his right hand toward the scientist. The scientist, still frowning, accepted the handshake and walked around Max toward one of the cages.

"I wasn't told of any newbies heading our way," said the scientist.

"Well, perhaps you missed the memo," replied Max. He waited a few seconds to see if the scientist would buy his lie. He was prepared to perform his kick-to-the-gut again.

The scientist eyed the coat in Max's hand and then opened one of the cages and retrieved a medium-sized rat. Max squirmed—he never did like those nasty animals.

"Well," said the scientist, "it's about time we have more help around here. Personally, I'm sick of the 'around-the-clock' hours. I don't care what the pay is."

Max relaxed his shoulders, and then put on the lab coat. He watched as the scientist pulled out a syringe from his coat pocket and injected a light blue fluid into the rat's side.

"So where are you from?" asked the scientist as he put the rat back into the cage.

Max perked up. "New York."

"Oh, really? Which part?"

"Queens. You know, I have to hit the can. Can you direct me?" asked Max.

"Down the hall to the right. You'll see the sign," answered the scientist as he jotted down notes on a tablet.

"Thanks," Max said. Holding the files under his right arm, he made his way to the main foyer of the building. There were plenty of people walking around, getting on and off the elevators, and sitting on couches talking on cell phones. The receptionist was typing on her computer.

No one seemed startled by his presence, so Max walked toward the large glass doors as if he had walked through this foyer thousands of times before.

Josh was flying.

"Dude, don't wanna a ticket right now," said Chris as he looked at his passenger side mirror.

"We're fine. Here's my cell phone. Try calling up Max."

"Gotcha," said Chris. He dialed Max's. "Max!"

"Yeah, who is this? Chris?" asked Max.

"Yes, where are you? Are you OK?"

"I'm fine. I'm at some kind of chemical laboratory called BioTech Worldwide. I've escaped, but they are holding the missing children here somewhere. Let the authorities there know what's going on."

"Great! OK, we will, but Josh and I are already on our way to Houston. Stella got your text," replied Chris.

"Good. Come get me. I'll meet you at the corner of Market and Fidelity on the east side near 610." Max put his cell in his pocket and took off the lab coat. He found a trash can on the side of the street, stuffed the coat inside, and headed for the rendezvous.

Josh dialed Stella on his phone. "Stella, it's Josh."

"Josh! Are you in Houston, yet?"

"Almost. We just crossed over the Beltway. Listen, we got a hold of Max, and he's fine. He escaped."

"Oh, thank God!" shouted Stella. "Where is he?"

"We're going to pick him up now. He mentioned a placed called BioTech Worldwide. Do you know anything about this?"

"No. Never heard of it," answered Stella.

"Stella, you better tell the police there what's going on," instructed Josh.

"I will, Josh. But do whatever Max says. Trust him—he knows what he's doing."

"I will. Hey—"

"Yeah?" replied Stella.

Josh paused for a couple of seconds, and then asked, "Is Rachel with you?"

"Yes, she's right here. Why?"

"Well, do you know if she's seeing anyone?"

"Josh! Just be careful." She hung up and rolled her eyes.

Josh set his phone on the console when Chris spoke up, "You know, Josh, it's really interesting."

"What is?"

"Why we are doing this. We're doing this—really—for those kids."

Josh looked at Chris. He was a little confused. "What do you mean?"

"I know we've set out to save Max, but what we're really trying to do is save these kids."

"Yeah, I see your point." Josh paused for a couple of seconds before asking, "But what's your point?"

"Well, we don't know what's going to happen when we pick up Max! What if the bad guys are watching him—waiting for us? What if they try to kill us? We're risking our lives to save children we've never met."

Chris stared out his window in thought. Then he continued, "I don't even know what they look like. I mean—think about it. You risked your life to save my family, but you know me. We don't know these kids."

"So what exactly are you getting at?" asked Josh.

Chris turned to his brother and asked, "These guys—whoever they are—are willing to do whatever it takes to get these kids. Are we willing to do whatever it takes to reach 'em first?"

Josh glanced at Chris. Then back to the road. He was silent as he drove his truck 100 miles per hour down I10.

CHAPTER NINE

Rachel stood at the foot of Isabella's hospital bed—tears rolling down her face. Why did this happen? How could this happen? How could fourteen children be mysteriously unharmed but one child end up like this?

These thoughts traveled through her mind. Then she wondered how the kidnappers knew where she and the orphans would be so they could take the children when the bus wrecked. Who else knew they were traveling to Houston? And did they cause the wreck?

Suddenly, a thought came to her mind—a possibility. No, it couldn't be! Could it?

She battled the thoughts. Surely he wouldn't be the culprit who tipped off the kidnappers! But no one else knew. She began to cry.

Her mind was on overload. Goosebumps formed all over her arms. Beads of sweat appeared on her forehead. Suddenly, from deep within the corridors of her brain, she heard some sort of electrical snap.

She closed her eyes, and her weeping ceased. She grabbed the bar at the end of Isabella's bed and began to squeeze tightly. Her countenance grew cold and dim, and her tears turned to ashes of bitter anger that seeped from her eyes. Her hands and legs began to shake, and her breathing pattern increased as her heart rate rose.

She opened her eyes, and the bitterness caused her eyes to redden. Her muscles hardened like a rock, and she appeared as one trained and ready to kill. Her easy temperament was erased and replaced with an inner untamable violence. Staring at Isabella, she clinched her teeth, turned away from the bed, and stormed out of the room.

Like a semi she walked down the hospital's hallway. A doctor was viewing his chart as Rachel's shoulder met his—throwing him off balance. He dropped his chart and watched with confusion as Rachel continued her warrior march.

A nurse attempted to catch her attention, but Rachel's demonic demeanor quickly submarined the nurse's words. She fearfully backed away, allowing Rachel to pass.

Rachel entered the hospital's main lobby and exited through the automatic sliding doors; a handful of nurses and doctors watched as she left. As she walked into the street, they began to call for her to stop. She stood directly in front of a white sedan until it came to a screeching halt just before hitting her.

Rachel walked to the driver's side, opened the door, grabbed the woman from behind the wheel, and threw her onto the side of the street. Then she got into the car and drove away.

Stella came running out of the hospital in total confusion. Three men also walked out and ordered the doctors and nurses to reenter the main lobby. As soon as everyone was back inside, the men called the medical group together.

One of them revealed his identity, "My name's Lee Tyler; I'm a special agent with the FBI. My partners and I were sent to protect the rest of the children. I know your day just went from bad to worse. We are here to help you, and by doing so, we will be taking custody of these children."

"Where will you be taking them?" one of the doctors asked.

"I'm sorry, Ma'am. That information is classified," said Agent Tyler.

Within minutes, all eleven children were escorted by armed FBI agents into three different minivans and taken away from the Lake Charles Memorial Hospital.

Josh pulled his truck into a small parking lot on the corner of Market and Fidelity Streets in Houston. Max opened the back passenger door and got into the back seat. However, just as they were about to drive off, several black cars with sirens and lights pulled in front of them, blocking their path.

"What is this?" shouted Chris.

"Max, what do I do?" asked Josh.

Max was amazingly calm. "Just stop and wait here." He got out, held up his hands, and walked in front of Josh's truck. Josh and Chris couldn't believe what was happening. They watched as men exited the black vehicles and approached Max. None of them had any weapons drawn, but one of them began talking with Max. He appeared to be the leader. There were about ten other men around Max watching and listening.

Then the man reached out and picked something off the back of Max's shoulder and showed it to him. Josh looked at Chris with a confused face.

Max began talking more. He was waving his hands in gesture—apparently explaining something big. The man he was talking with did not appear happy.

After about five more minutes, Josh couldn't sit still anymore. He got out of the truck and began to walk toward the men. The men stopped talking and stared at Josh as he approached. Josh began to wonder whether or not he was in a dream.

Max spoke up, "It's alright; he's with me."

Then the man who was talking with Max ordered to his men, "Alright. Fine. Let's do this."

Max turned to Josh, "Josh, you and Chris are going to ride with these men. They're FBI. Don't worry; everything will be just fine."

With that, Max got into one of the black cars, and all but one drove off. Then Chris jumped out of the truck and asked, "Hey, what's going on here? Where's Max going?"

The two men who stayed behind told them to get inside their car. "We'll explain everything on the way," said the driver.

Stella was beside herself. Completely exhausted and confused, she sat in the hospital's main waiting room with her head in her hands. She hadn't heard from Max; she didn't even know whether or not he was alive.

Rachel had turned into something she'd never seen before, and she feared what would happen to her—or anyone with whom she came in contact. Naomi was still in critical condition, but she was at least stabilized. And the children were taken away to who-knows-where.

She missed the days when it was only hurricanes that troubled her life. All she wanted to do now was sleep, but she felt too afraid to make herself that vulnerable in public. Her nerves were frayed. She felt danger lurking around her.

As she sat with her eyes closed, she heard the main sliding doors open, and the sound of footsteps grow louder as someone approached her. She was too tired to see who it was; if it was really important to interrupt her, he or she would speak up.

And speak up he did. "Excuse me, Mrs. McClain. I need you to come with me."

Stella slowly raised her head. Her dark, brown hair fell into her face—blocking her view. She moved her hair and looked at the man who instructed her. Then her eyes widened with fear.

"My name is Agent Wright. I believe we've met."

"Alright, I need one of you to tell us what's going on. I want answers. And where are you taking us!" Chris said as his temper was about to get the best of him. "I've had quite a bit of stress these last few weeks."

"Sure, Mr. Sonnier. Mr. McClain suggested we tell you two everything," replied the agent in the front passenger seat.

Josh quickly looked at Chris, as if saying, "How did he know your name?"

The agent began his story, "Fifteen years ago we intercepted a middle eastern trade vessel off the coast of Libya. Inside were 34 undocumented children who, we later found out, were all from the same Swedish village. They each had been experimented upon—some with a mind control technique called IMI, or Intelligence-manned Interface. It's some sort of microchip injected in the neck where, in theory, they could be controlled offsite by a supercomputer."

"We were never able to find out who the mastermind behind all this was, but about six months ago we received a tip about a Russian scientist named, Vladimir Sokolov. Apparently, he'd been hired by someone inside Libya to conduct experiments on people for military enhancement purposes. We think this has to do with the children from Sweden fifteen years ago. We also think it has to do with the orphans from Peru."

"OK. Whoa. This is huge," said Chris.

"So this Russian dude wants Peruvian orphans to help him with military enhancement in Libya. I don't get it," interjected Josh.

"And neither did we," replied the agent, "until we began to piece things together. Those kids from that Swedish village all had the same strange and rare condition called congenital analgesia. Another word for it is CIP—congenital insensitivity to pain. Dr. Sokolov, apparently, conducted experiments on those poor children so he could formulate a concoction that would make soldiers painfree in battle. He would make millions—billions, even."

Josh interrupted, "And the orphans from Peru—they don't experience pain?"

"Well, that's the problem. We believe he wants the Peruvian orphans for this purpose—he, obviously, thinks they have this CIP condition. But what he doesn't know is that they are different. They are not just painfree. They are totally injury free." After the agent made that last remark, the car was silent.

The driver finally spoke up, "It's way beyond us."

Josh and Chris sat in the back, stunned. Russian mad scientists, Swedish villages, Peruvian orphans—this seemed like a worldwide mystery movie.

"OK, but where does Max fit into all this?" Josh asked.

The two agents briefly looked at one another, perhaps each hoping for the other to answer the question. Finally, the driver answered, "We'll talk more when we get to the station."

"You're taking us to the FBI Headquarters? Cool!" yelled Chris ecstatically.

The white sedan parked directly in front of BioTech Worldwide, and Rachel got out of the car. She burst through the main doors and headed for the elevators. Two men attempted to board the elevators, as well. They noticed Rachel and her red, demon-like eyes. She shook her head, and they abruptly stopped and backed off. The doors closed.

The receptionist noticed Rachel and picked up her phone, "Sir, I think she's here."

"Good. We are ready," said the man on the other end.

The elevator doors opened, and Rachel walked down a long hall. She felt like she had been here before—she knew right where to go. Her thoughts were at war with each another. It was as if she hated what she was doing, but something inside her told her to continue. And her anger was incredibly deep-seeded.

She rounded a corner of the hall and saw large, wooden, double doors straight ahead. Without pausing, she burst through the doors and walked past the office secretary who wasn't about to voice a complaint to her.

Suddenly, her eyes widened. It was him. She had hoped she would never see his face again. Fear paralyzed her. Her mind wouldn't utter a single thought. There was another man standing nearby, but his back was toward her.

Then he turned slowly to face her.

Rob Emanual.

The fear exited her mind. She twisted back to her right and thrust forward with all her might—jacking Rob square in the jaw. The impact sent him tumbling over the office guest chair in front of Sokolov's desk and landing hard on the floor. Rob moved slowly to his feet—rubbing his face and moaning.

"It is good to have you back, Rachel!" exclaimed Dr. Sokolov in his infamous Russian accent.

CHAPTER TEN

Dale Jackson was amazed at the outpouring of compassion from the churches in Caroline Springs, Louisiana. The pastors were meeting with her at Camp Pinerock's conference room to discuss partnerships with Child Evangelism Fellowship, so they could be trained to reach out to children in their communities.

"There are apartment complexes, elementary public schools, neighborhoods, trailer parks—so many areas where CEF can train you to effectively reach children. And then, once you reach the children, you can reach the whole family," she said to the pastors.

"So, Dale, explain to us the partnership procedure. What do we do?" asked Mike.

Dale handed out a document that clarified CEF's statement of faith to each pastor. "If you can sign on the dotted line at the bottom, saying that you agree with this statement of faith, we'll get right to work. In order for us to be effective we gotta be on the same page," she explained. "What's most important is that we are all clear on the gospel: Christ died for our sins and rose from the dead. Trusting in Him, alone, saves us for eternity."

Each pastor read through the statement and signed. Then Dale said, "So we're all ready. Our trainers can come to your facilities and teach you all you need to know to get started. What we need now is to set up times. So who wants to go first?"

Immediately, all hands and voices were raised by the pastors. Dale sat down in awe. She had never seen such a desire by pastors to be as aggressive in outreach evangelism. She quieted down the crew and began to organize them into groups for training.

Charlie Metcalf approached Dale. He seemed a bit cautious, "Mrs. Jackson, may I ask you a question?"

"Sure, anything."

"My son and I would like to participate, but we haven't done much with children before. And to be honest, we haven't ever shared the gospel with anyone. So this is very new to us. I'm actually a tad bit nervous about this whole thing. No—I'm actually very nervous."

"I understand, Mr. Metcalf, but I—"

"Mrs. Jackson, I'm terrified. I've been terrified all my life—I mean, since I became a Christian—of telling people about Jesus. Can your training help me?"

"Mr. Metcalf," Dale said smiling, "let me first say that I appreciate your honesty. Your transparency is refreshing, and I want you to know that you are not alone. Most people who go through our training begin with the exact same feelings as you do. I think you'll do just fine. It's God Who brings the power—we just follow Him in obedience."

"Well, how do I know I'm being obedient? I've never led anyone to Christ," said Charlie.

"Mr. Metcalf, you're here, aren't you?" responded Dale.

Charlie smiled, nodded, and sat back down in his chair. His thoughts turned toward those unmet children throughout their parish. In his mind's eye, he could see dozens of children laughing and playing. Then they all turned to him and watched as he spoke. He could see them praying. He could see little chains fall, tears drop, and joyful sounds echoing out of heaven. He opened his eyes—he was ready to reach those unknown children.

Josh and Chris sat in a small conference room waiting for the agents. The respect they had for Max was very high, yet they were somewhat confused and even a little upset that something was kept from them.

"Do you think Max is in trouble?" asked Chris. Josh sat next to him slightly tilting his Styrofoam cup, carefully making his coffee swish back and forth.

He sighed and answered, "I dunno. I don't think so. The way he willingly went with them—it almost seemed like they were following him."

"Yeah, well, I don't like this. What does the FBI need with Max? What does he have to do with these kidnapped kids from Peru?" Chris said.

Just then, the door opened and in walked the two agents who brought them there. One of them sat while the other stood by the door.

"Hi, guys. My name is Special Agent Nick Daniels. I used to work with Max McClain when he was here."

Josh tilted his head. "When he was here? Max worked for the FBI?"

Agent Daniels sat back in his chair. "You don't know much about Special Agent McClain, do you?"

Josh and Chris looked at each other, and then Chris interjected, "Fill us in."

Agent Daniels complied, "Max was one of the best here. His background, before he joined the FBI, was remarkable." The agent opened a manila folder with documents and pictures. "Here, he asked me to show you these."

The documents revealed an incredible array of accomplishments: Navy SEALs, B.S. in Criminal Justice, and fifteen years as a special agent in the FBI.

"He was a Navy SEAL?" asked Chris.

"He was special ops, yes. He was on the SEAL team that went into Iraq in '91 ahead of the American Forces to keep an eye on Saddam prior to the invasion force."

Josh and Chris flipped through the documents and pictures as Daniels continued. "He had strict orders to take out Saddam if his forces put up any kind of fight. Max knew what Saddam had for breakfast, lunch, and dinner. And he also knew which son was going to take over the country if Saddam died of natural or unnatural causes."

Josh sat back and stared at the agent.

"He was very good," said Daniels. "He was the Special Agent-in-charge before he retired a couple years ago."

"I knew he had worked for the government, but I didn't know all of this," Josh said. "Why was this kept secret?"

"Max was involved in many top secret missions. Most of them—well, only a few of the top dogs around here knew about."

"What top secret missions," asked Chris.

"Well, the ones that are top secret," replied Daniels rather sarcastically. Chris sat back in frustration.

"So why do you need him now?" asked Josh.

The agent standing next to the door spoke up and walked toward the table where the men were sitting, "Remember that trade vessel we told you about on the way here? Special Agent McClain unfolded the mystery as to why those Swedish children were experimented on. He uncovered some nasty secrets from a small Russian band and a couple other Middle Eastern countries.

"He helped us identify Dr. Vladimir Sokolov, the Russian scientist who experimented on those kids and many others. We think he's been hired by a terrorist country. Special Agent McClain knows Sokolov better than anyone else."

"The main reason we need him," Agent Daniels interjected, "is because he's that good. And right now, we need him to help us locate those kidnapped orphans."

"So where are they now?" asked Chris.

"Our supervising agent is leading a team to recover the children. They're back at the BioTech Lab. Max is with them," Daniels answered.

Three FBI units convened in an empty parking lot across from BioTech. Several well-armed agents were suiting up.

Special Agent-in-Charge Brian Nichols approached Max with his hand extended. "McClain, you doing OK?" he said.

"I've had my better moments," Max replied, shaking Nichols' hand.

"Listen, Max, just to let you know—I was not the one who decided to bring you into this, but you need to understand that I am still in charge with this operation. You do nothing except by my permission only. Am I clear?" demanded Nichols.

"Sure, that's fine. Tell me what you want me to do." said Max humbly. Nichols barked out a few orders to his men and then handed Max a vest and a .40 caliber Glock.

Nichols looked straight at Max, realizing that Max wouldn't agree with his plan. "We're going in."

"Brian, can I have a word with you?" Max asked Nichols. The two stepped aside from the rest of the agents.

"What is it, McClain?" said Nichols sternly.

"I appreciate your forward approach into the building, but may I suggest—"

"I don't need any of your suggestions," Nichols said with his pointer finger in Max's face. "You're not FBI, anymore, Max. We're just borrowing you for this one operation." With that, Nichols turned to his men and ordered them to move ahead.

Dr. Sokolov commanded three armed men to stand guard outside his lab. He closed the door behind him and walked over to a large metal container. He keyed in 6 numbers on a digital keypad, and the container opened with a thick, white cloud spewing out from the liquid nitrogen cases inside.

He lifted a small door that revealed an electronic device. He pressed a green button, and the red LED lights lit up on the device. The Russian keyed in 10:00 on the device and carefully closed it. He walked out of the lab with his mob surrounding him.

Pistols were drawn. The lobby was empty. Max and the other special agents carefully made their way into the interior of BioTech Worldwide.

The Russian and his three men walked up to a holding room, and one of the men unlocked and opened the door. There were four dark-skinned children inside.

"Let's go," demanded Dr. Sokolov.

The armed men escorted Sokolov and the children to the roof of the building where a helicopter awaited them.

"You three take care of our guests. Make sure they enter the lab. In exactly eight minutes, you want to run for your lives, yes?"

Max and his men walked down the same long hallway Max had been in before. This time they were there for a purpose. Max wanted those children.

Suddenly, a smoke bomb was thrown in their direction!

Max shouted, "Take cover!"

6 minutes

Shots were fired! A bullet pierced an agent's shoulder, and Max pulled him off to the side. "Don't shoot until you see something!" he shouted.

Then he heard the sound of a helicopter. Max took his chance. "To the roof! Go to the roof!"

Max led the way into the smoke. He saw a glimpse of movement to his left and fired. One of Sokolov's men fell. Max made a fast left--his men were on his tail. He moved his 57-year-old legs as fast as he could.

Another man jumped out from the right and took a shot. The bullet grazed Max's right shoulder, and a federal agent took out the man from behind Max.

5 minutes

Max didn't stop. He ran up the flight of stairs to the roof. Just as they burst through the door, Max saw the Russian and four Peruvian children inside the helicopter. They had just taken off. But Max looked more closely inside and spotted two more figures: a man and a woman.

"No way," he said out loud. It was Rachel Willard and Rob Emanual. It was Rob's name he saw in the file, but he had no idea that Rachel was in on this, too.

Max stood there and watched as the helicopter flew away. Just then, one of his agents shouted, "Sir! We found a bomb! Evacuate now!"

4 minutes

Max dashed back into the building, all the while yelling for his agents to escape. He kept each man in front of him, and he grabbed the wounded agent to carry him out.

There were two agents directly in front of Max. All were dashing toward the main lobby. Suddenly, a bullet hit the wall just to Max's right. He handed off the wounded agent and told them to exit the building.

"Three minutes, Max!" shouted the agent as he carried off his wounded partner.

3 minutes

Shots came from behind Max, but smoke still blinded the hallway. Max hid around a corner on the right and returned fire. Then he checked his gun. Six rounds left.

2 minutes

Out of nowhere the man jumped from around the corner. Hand to hand combat ensued, knocking the guns from their hands. Max hadn't fought like this in over two years. He took two hits to face but blocked the next three.

Max swung a right hook, but missed and took another punch to the gut and another to the head. That sent him to the ground. He quickly jumped up and got a good look at his target. He noticed a familiar tattoo on the man's left wrist. He looked straight into the man's eyes and waited for his next move.

The man lunged for Max, but Max rejected and used his opponent's momentum to throw him against the wall. Max thrust forward a right elbow dislocating the man's jaw. He threw his left fist to his ribcage, and then his right first to his sternum. The force of the blows to the man up against the wall caused his bones to crack. He could barely breathe, and he couldn't speak.

20 seconds

Max charged him with his head down and picked him up over his shoulder. Then he ran hard through the front doors. Max made a fast dash for parked cars in the lot where they could hide from the coming blast.

A shock wave blew Max forward several feet, and he dropped the man he was carrying. The wave was followed by the deep, ear-popping force of the explosion behind him. His opponent was slammed into one of the parked cars, knocking him unconscious. Max grabbed the man and dragged him behind a car, while debris from the exploded building flew by and fell around them.

In a matter of minutes, dozens of fire trucks, ambulances, and law enforcement surrounded the area. Max sat in the back of an ambulance while paramedics checked him out. When he saw his opponent on a stretcher, he slowly made his way to him.

"Is he conscious?" Max asked the paramedic standing next to him.

"He is now, but we have to quickly get him to the hospital," the paramedic responded.

Max leaned into his opponent's face, placed his hand on one of his cracked ribs, and asked one question, "Where is he taking the children?"

The man's eyes widened. Just a little pressure on his broken ribs shot pain all through his body. He immediately answered in a very nervous Middle-eastern accent, "He has place north of Conroe. Very wooded—hard to find."

Max pushed a little on the man's ribs, and the man groaned in pain. Then he shouted, "I have address! I give you address!" Max released his pressure and turned around just in time to see his wife running toward him.

In the background was Agent Dwayne Wright closing the car door in which they had just arrived. Stella jumped into her husband's arms.

"Are you OK?" she shouted.

He kissed her and responded, "I am, but this isn't over."

Max grabbed her hand and made his way through the crowd toward Special Agent Nichols.

"Did you get the chopper?" Max asked Nichols.

"We're working on it. How are you?"

"I'm fine, but there's more to this than we had realized." Max turned to Stella and continued, "I saw Rachel with him. Rob Emmanuel was with him, too. Stella, it looks as though Rob and Christa were in on this."

"What?" shouted Stella. "And Rachel?"

"I don't know. The look on her face—she didn't look like a kidnapped victim to me," responded Max. "But there's more," he turned to Nichols. "I didn't think about this before, but those documents I gave you—the ones I took from the lab—they mentioned a list of names. They were names of married couples who were applying for adoption. Some of them had the word eligible stamped next to their names, as well as the sum of $100,000."

Nichols squinted his eyes at Max.

"You don't—you don't get it," Max said. "Sokolov was trying to pay off some of these couples to adopt a child so he could take them and perform his experiments. Rob and Christa Emmanuel were on that list. That's how I know they were involved. Sokolov wants the list that I've hidden so he can go after the rest."

"Do you still have the list?" asked Nichols.

"Not in my possession, but I can get it. What I can't figure out is how I escaped the lab so easily."

"Oh, that. Yes, I forgot to tell you," Nichols said. "That was us. Daniels and Wright work for me."

Max stared at Nichols for a couple seconds. Nichols' eyes widened. Max took two steps toward him. Nichols gasped, held up his hands, and said, "Now, Max. Let me explain."

Calmly, Max replied, "Explain, then."

Nichols breathed deeply. Nervously he said, "We needed to place you in the lab, because we knew you could retrieve the intel we were looking for. Daniels and Wright were in, but could only go so far. Sokolov wouldn't let them close enough. We needed to move fast, so we used you. Hope you don't mind." Nichols smiled sheepishly.

"You scared my wife and staff."

"Hey, we needed you to believe they were working for Sokolov. We believed you wouldn't have helped us if we'd just ask."

"Sir," interjected an approaching agent, "we have the address. Local authority spotted a chopper in the vicinity."

Nichols looked to Max.

"Fine," Max said calmly. Then he took one step closer to Nichols. The men were standing face to face. "This time I need you to listen to my suggestions."

The helicopter landed in the large front yard of Sokolov's States-side home just north of Conroe. It was an old farmhouse he had acquired a few years ago. He, a few armed men, four children, Rob, and Rachel exited the helicopter and ran toward the house's front entry where a maid stood with the door opened to welcome them.

The armed men led the group into the living room. The house had an antique feel with an squeaky wooden floor, and furniture that appeared to have been sitting for a hundred years.

The men instructed Rob, Rachel, and the children to sit in the living room. Two maids brought hot food for the guests. As the children devoured their meal, Rob watched with wonder at the poor kids—they were so innocent. He rubbed his forehead and temples.

He looked at the children. Two of them were staring back. They had big, dark brown eyes that penetrated his heart, and his heart couldn't take much more shame.

He pictured his own children in his mind. The hurricane. The rising water. The near death experience as he chipped away the roof from inside the attic—escaping just in time to save the lives of his wife and children.

Now he was part of a scheme to endanger the lives of innocent Peruvian orphans—children who have never experienced the feeling of being loved by a mother and father. It was at that moment—looking into the precious eyes of these children as they ate—that he decided to make this right. He didn't know what he would do, but he knew he had to do something.

He was startled when the oldest orphan spoke to him in Spanish, "Are you going to hurt us?"

Fluent in their language, Rob felt his eyes swell with tears, and a severe lump formed in his throat. "No, no! In fact," Rob looked toward the doorway, "I'm going to try to get you out of here. Don't worry. Everything will be OK."

Half an hour passed, and the armed men led the children to a holding room with locked doors and windows. As the men walked back to the living room, Rob stood up as if to say something. Just then, the front door opened. One of the front guards stood there looking at Dr. Sokolov with wide eyes.

"What is it?" asked Sokolov.

"It's McClain. He's here," answered the guard.

"What?" Sokolov rushed to the window, as did 2 of his men.

"He's just walking down the drive toward the house," explained the guard.

Rob felt a sudden rush of nausea. Beads of sweat appeared on his forehead. He thought about taking the chance to escape, but he didn't want to leave the children. He stood watching—waiting for Max to arrive.

Max was alone, carrying only a briefcase in his right hand. He calmly approached the old house. Rob's hands were shaking, and his palms were sweaty. His eyes were locked on the front door. He heard the sound of footsteps on the front porch. The friend he had betrayed—the one who gave so much—was about to realize who he really was.

The door opened. The guards, at the instruction of Sokolov, allowed Max to enter. Max walked into the living room, looked at Rob, but then approached Sokolov.

"Hello, Max," Sokolov said.

"Vladimir," responded Max.

"It has been a while."

"Fifteen years, if you count the two you had me imprisoned."

"Yes," said Sokolov as he reached for a cigar, "that was a tough time. My apologies for the way you were treated."

"You mean the way I was tortured?"

As Sokolov lit his cigar, he noticed burn scars on Max's right hand. He recalled the yells of a man tortured in a dark cell. Then he sat down in an old, cushioned chair. "You look well," he said, keeping an eye on the brief case. "Please, have a seat."

"I'd rather stand."

Sokolov gracefully nodded, puffed his cigar and asked, "And what do we have in the case? A bomb, perhaps?"

"If I wanted you dead, I would have killed you long ago," said Max. He placed the briefcase on the coffee table. He began to unzip the sides to open it. Just then, one of the guards interrupted, "Sir! I must protest!"

"Please, please, Filipp," responded Sokolov calmly. "Mr. McClain wants to present us with something. He has no desire for harm. By all means, Max, continue." Sokolov puffed his cigar and watched as Max opened the case.

He pulled out a laptop, placed it on the table, and opened it. It beeped as it rebooted from its hibernation. Max pressed a few keys, and a video popped up. There was a beautiful young, blonde with a very sad countenance.

Suddenly, Sokolov became very serious. He immediately placed his cigar on the table and stood to his feet.

"What is this?" he asked. He turned toward Max, "You would not dare hurt her."

"Sit down. Please." Sokolov hestitated for a second before returning to his seat. Max continued, "How long has it been since you've seen your daughter?"

Sokolov stared at the screen and then looked at Max. "You would not hurt her."

"How long has it been?" Max repeated forcefully.

Sokolov sat quietly for a few seconds before answering. "Three years. It has been three years since her mother passed. I have not seen my Natalya since then."

"And why is that?"

"Because she blames me for her mother's death!" It was silent. Max waited. Sokolov finally broke the silence with a quivering voice, "I suppose you want to make bargain, but I—I cannot."

"Your daughter is safe, Vladimir. We have no desire to hurt her."

"Then why are you here?" asked the Russian curiously.

Max leaned over the laptop and pressed a button which played the video.

Papa, why do you do this? Why did you leave me? I have not seen you in over three years. I have searched for you. Just to hear your voice. I am not angry at you anymore!

Papa, I don't understand. Why do you take these children? I don't understand what is going on, Papa. They say you have committed crimes. Serious crimes! They say you—are hurting innocent people—children!

Please stop, Papa. Please! Stop this! And come home to me! I miss you—I need you, Papa. I love you! Papa, do you understand? I love you!

Sokolov stared at the screen. He closed his eyes tightly and the tears flowed.

He had brief flashbacks of his daughter as a little girl. How he missed those days. Now, he had entered into a life where he was left with no choices.

"Max, you do not know what you are doing. I cannot stop what I do. They are watching."

"Who, Vladimir? Who is watching?" asked Max as he slammed shut the laptop.

Rob walked out of the living room toward the holding area where the children were being kept.

Sokolov noticed Rob's exit, but looked up to Max with tear-filled eyes. He realized he was in too deep. His emotions were beginning to overtake him.

"I know they're Libyan," Max said. "I saw the tattoo on the one who attacked me at your lab. The crescent moon and star. Tell me who is running this operation. Just give me a name, Vladimir. That's all I want." Sokolov sat with thought, and then he looked at Max.

"Three years ago, a man named Amir Nasab contacted me with a most profitable offer. I had already been working on a project called Geroi. It was still in experimental stages, but I began to become successful at enhancing our soldiers in Russia. We were on the verge of creating the supersoldier, Max! Mother Russia would, once again, become the superpower she was destined to be.

"Part of the project included my ability to create a formula that enabled them to feel no pain, thus removing much fear in battle. However, after about a year, the test soldiers began to show signs of deterioration of the joints. Then their bone marrow began to breakdown. My formula did not work, and the Russian government discontinued funding."

"That's when Nasab contacted you," Max guessed.

"He offered me a substantial amount of money for continuing my work," replied Sokolov. "At first, I refused. I knew he was a terrorist, and I did not wish to be in that line of work any longer.

Sokolov looked at Max's scared hand again. Then he looked into his eyes and said, "I remember well what we did to you, McClain. I am truly sorry."

Max didn't make a sound. Sokolov continued.

"So he take my wife and murder her." Sokolov broke down and wept. Max sat down in the chair across from him. The guards looked on with awe at their superior in such a form.

"They kill her, and then told me they would do the same to Natalya if I did not adhere to their commands." Sokolov looked up at Max. "Nasab murder my beautiful wife. To this day, Natalya does not know this. I must finish this job to keep her alive. So you see, Max, just the fact that you have approached her to make this video to persuade me has put her life in more jeopardy."

Rob walked up and saw Afon Sokolov open the door of the room where the Peruvian orphans were.

"What are you doing?" Rob asked.

"What does it look like? I stood at the entrance of the room listening to my father being weakened by this American. I am taking the children back to Russia, myself."

Rob waited for Afon to face the door, and then he picked up a pipe lying nearby. He raised it to hit Afon, but Afon noticed and charged into him before Rob could swing the pipe.

The two wrestled on the ground. Rob was able to pin him down. He laid two good hits, but Afon grabbed Rob's head with his left hand and pushed him off to the side. Then he pulled out a knife.

Back in the living room, Max leaned over the desk where Sokolov sat and pleaded, "Listen, Vladimir, we can protect your daughter. Help us help you. I know Nasab. I've run into him before. You have to bring us to him!"

"You must understand, Max. I need those children to save my daughter."

"Those children do not have CIP, Vladimir!" Max pounded on the table as he shouted.

Sokolov stared at Max.

Max stood up and continued more calmly, "They have nothing to do with your experiments. They are normal children, except they have no families. No one to love them. No one to raise them, nurture them, care for them—and you are taking away every opportunity they might have to receive those things they need."

Max stepped closer to Sokolov and lowered his voice. "What you are doing to these children, Vladimir, is exactly what you don't want to be done to your own daughter." Sokolov kept his gaze fixed on Max. "You must see this irony," Max continued. "You must see that what you are doing to these children is just as evil as what those Libyan mercenaries are threatening to do to Natalya."

Sokolov had a distasteful frown. He looked down at the floor and said, "How do you know they do not have CIP? The reports I have been given stated that they feel no pain."

"They've been checked out. They are normal. They just—I don't know—they don't experience injury. They're not just pain free, they are injury free." Max stared at Sokolov, hoping and praying that he was getting through to him. "Sokolov, you must stop this. You must let us help you and Natalya. You must lead us to Nasab."

Suddenly, there was a loud thump coming from a different part of the house. Sokolov got up from his chair.

Max asked, "What was that?"

"That came from the direction of the children's room."

"Where is your son?"

"Afon," replied Sokolov. "Max, he try to take children! Follow me!"

CHAPTER ELEVEN

Afon Sokolov slid into the driver's seat of the white Dodge Grand Caravan. In the back were the four children, Rachel, and one armed, Libyan mercenary.

As they approached the main road from the long driveway, two black FBI units pulled in to block him. He floored the gas pedal and plowed through the road block. Then the Libyan, sitting in the front passenger seat, opened his window and fired an Uzi at the FBI units behind them, blowing out two tires on one unit and one tire on the other one.

The FBI agents didn't return fire. The children were at risk, so they allowed the van to escape. Agent Nichols radioed into HQ that the children were on the move.

Josh and Chris sat in the office of the Federal Bureau of Investigation in Houston. The boredom was killing them, and Josh badly wanted to do something to help Max. Just then, the commotion of several agents and office workers caught their attention.

Chris looked at Josh. "I'm gonna try to get close enough to hear," he said. He made his way toward the scuffling agents. Some were on their phones, while others were scanning computer screens and speaking in FBI jargon that was unfamiliar to Chris.

He walked toward a water cooler and poured himself a drink. As he sipped, he picked up on a few words from the several conversations. Then he walked back to Josh.

"What'd you here?" asked Josh.

"I don't know what all's going on, but it seems the children have been moved. I think Max has that Russian dude, though."

Josh stood up. "This is ridiculous," he said with frustration.

"What are you doing?" asked Chris.

Josh walked directly up to an agent. "Excuse me, what's going on here. Is Max OK?"

The agent didn't look up from his computer screen as he answered, "Yeah, he's OK. But the kids have been taken by someone else."

"Who?"

The agent looked up at Josh with a raise eyebrow. "We'll handle it, son."

Sokolov led Max down the hall toward the holding area. Max saw someone lying down on the floor.

"No," whispered Max, and he ran over to the body.

Kneeling down, Max gazed upon his friend. "No. Jesus, no. Please."

Rob was bleeding badly from his abdomen. Slowly, he opened his eyes. "Max," he said quietly.

Max couldn't believe he was still alive. He had lost a lot of blood.

"Max, I'm so sorry," Rob said.

"Shhh. Just rest. We're gonna get you to a hospital soon."

"Max, I'm so sorry. I want you to know—" Rob stiffed his jaw and moaned in pain.

"Rob, don't talk. I understand."

"No, I need to say—I believe. I believe everything you told me. I wanted to get out of this."

Max's eyes filled with tears. He knew his friend was about to breathe his last. He had seen many deaths, but this one really hurt.

"You were right about grace. Forgiveness. Love. I want you to know that I believe you. I believe He died for me. I'm trusting Him alone."

Max forced a smile through his tears, "That's good, Rob. That's really good!"

"You are my friend, Max. You're my brother." He moaned again.

Rob was still for a few seconds. Max thought it was over. Then, with his watering eyes still closed, Rob asked, "Please help my family, Max. Please protect them."

"I will." Rob's breathing slowed. "Go home," whispered Max. "Go home." His breathing stopped. Max squeezed Rob's hand. He closed his eyes and prayed, "My Lord, He's Yours."

Max stood up slowly and looked at the Russian. He stood there staring at Max with horror on his face. Sokolov had opened the door to the room where the Peruvian orphans were being held. The room was empty. Sokolov said, "We're too late."

Max grabbed Sokolov's arm and squeezed tightly. "Where did he go?"

Sokolov didn't hesitate, "The Rusalka. She's a ship bound for Russia. She's harbored in Houston's port."

Max's countenance stiffened. Something was different. His walk was tight. Sokolov recalled Max's famed endurance of the torture he had forced on him fifteen years ago. The ability Max had to remain calm during the painful experiences during his imprisonment for two years was a phenomenon among the FBI.

But Max's demeanor was not calm now. He was stone cold. Hard. With Sokolov's right arm in the tight grasp of Max's hand, they walked out of the old farm house. Max was greeted with FBI agents in the front yard, and he released the Russian scientist into their custody.

"He will tell you where his son, Afon, is taking the children. Call it in," Max instructed. Max made his way to the back of one of the wrecked units and popped open the trunk. He grabbed a Glock .40 and four magazines, loading one into the pistol. Then he grabbed a vest and put it on.

One of the agents approached him in protest. "What are you doing?" Max looked at him. No words were spoken as the agent backed off.

Max grabbed two more pistols, closed the trunk, and walked to the driver's door of another unit. He opened the door and turned to the agent, "Call for backup. Houston port. The ship is called the Rusalka. I'll see you there."

The agent responded, "Yes, sir." Then he watched as Max drove away.

A special agent answered his desk phone at HQ. "Yes, sir. I understand. We're on our way." He hung up and shouted, "Listen up everyone! We have the location of where the children are being taken. We need two SWAT units to the Houston port immediately. Further instructions will be given on your radios while in route. Let's go, people! Let's go!"

The agent who talked with Josh just minutes before looked up to where the two boys were sitting. They were gone, so he went back to work.

Josh and Chris were already heading to the truck. They couldn't wait to be speeding down Loop 610. Josh dialed Max on his cell.

"Max, are you OK?"

"Yeah, I'm fine. Where's Stella?"

"She's good. I think she just stepped out to get something to eat," Josh said. "We overheard some talk about the children being moved to the Houston Port."

"Yeah, Sokolov's son took them before we could get to them. He plans to take them back to Russia."

"On board a ship?"

"Some ship called the Rusalka, but don't worry. We'll get to them before they depart. Just hang tight. I have to go, Josh."

"But wait, Max. Where have you been?"

"In Conroe. At an old farm house. It was Sokolov's hideout."

"A farm house? That's weird," replied Josh.

"Definitely a weird place. Nothing but old furniture and one room with a huge computer system. FBI will check it out. Josh, I gotta go. We'll talk more later."

Stella walked into the foyer of the FBI Headquarters. She rode the elevator to the floor where she, Josh, and Chris had been waiting. She walked into the large room where agents were working. She looked around for Josh and Chris but couldn't find them. A female agent walked toward her.

"Ma'am, can I help you?" the agent asked.

"Well, I'm looking for Josh Ward and Chris Sonnier. We were here waiting, but I can't seem to find them," answered Stella.

"It's OK," the agent said with a smile. "This is a big place. I'm sure they're around here somewhere. Can I get you some coffee?"

"No, that's OK. Thank you," answered Stella. "I'll just go back and sit down."

"Tengo miedo. Por favor, no nos hacen daño!" On board the Rusalka, one of the orphans spoke to Afon. She was scared and asked that they wouldn't be hurt.

"Molchi! Shut up!" yelled Afon. He led the group deep inside the ship.

Josh and Chris drove down the port, eyeing each ship for Russian wording. Finally, Chris spotted a cargo ship with giant Russian letters on the back. Underneath the letters was the word Rusalka. Enormous cranes were loading containers onto the ship's deck. They parked and quickly made their way to the ship and boarded it.

"Josh, what are we gonna do?" asked Chris. "We can't just go up to them and demand those kids."

Josh stopped, looked around, and then spoke softly to his brother. "Chris, you said earlier we must be willing to risk it all to save these orphans. Still willing?"

Chris took a deep breath and replied, "Lead the way."

Afon locked the children in a room and ordered the Libyan to stand guard. Then he handed the ship's captain a wad of cash.

"I want no trouble from you or your crew. Just get this boat moving soon," said Afon to the Captain.

Josh and Chris made their way below the stern. So far, they were able to avoid being seen. Chris' heart pounded. Suddenly, the ships horn sounded two short blasts, causing the boys to jump.

"What does that mean?" asked Chris.

"I'm not sure. I think it means we're about to leave. Come on."

They scurried around until they heard voices. Two Russian sailors were approaching, and their laughter was echoing through the long, metal corridor. Josh and Chris hid around the corner.

Josh thrust his right leg into the gut of one of the sailors. Chris finished him off with a fist to the face as Josh threw a right hook into the jaw of the other sailor. Then he grabbed the sailor, threw him to the floor, and demanded answers.

"Where are the children?" Josh said quietly, but sternly. "Tell me now!"

"I—I don't know! I don't know!" said the sailor with fear in his wide eyes.

"Josh, keep it down!" said Chris.

"Tell me where they are—I know you know where they are!" yelled Josh. Then he gave the sailor an elbow to the sternum. The sailor screamed in agony, and Josh covered his mouth to keep him as quiet as possible.

The sailor gave in. "OK! OK. They are in holding area behind engine room." Suddenly, the ship's engines started. Then they heard a voice from a handheld radio that was clipped on the side of the sailor. Josh grabbed it and yanked it off the sailor's belt. The language was in Russian, so Josh demanded the soldier to interpret.

"It's Afon Sokolov. He's the one who bring children. He says it is time to go," said the sailor. Josh and Chris tied and gagged them and then locked them inside a small supply closet.

"There's no way we can wait for the FBI, now," said Chris. "We have to move." Josh took a deep breath and rested his head against the wall behind him. He shook his right hand. It was sore from punching the sailor. He breathed deeply again, and prayed, "Lord, give us success for Your honor. Give us those children." His heart was pounding and his nerves were vibrating.

He and Chris began their trek down the corridors of the ship. Josh carefully peaked in every room. In one room, he noticed boxes of C4 explosives. "They should have a No Smoking sign above this door," joked Chris.

Just as they rounded a corner, they ran into a tall, slender man holding a radio. They froze, and the man tilted his head in wonder of who they were.

Josh didn't make a sound—he stood up straight and stared at the man. He wanted the man to speak first. The man made two steps to his right, and Josh stepped to his left in response. Finally, the man spoke in a thick Russian accent, "Who are you, and what are you doing here?"

Josh squinted his eyes as he recognized the voice from earlier on the radio. He switched his stance for attack. "It's him. It's Afon." he said. Afon's eyes got big. He saw the fierce determination in his opponent. But just as Josh was about to pounce on his enemy, he felt a shove from behind him. He turned his head quickly to see what happened—it was Chris. He was lying on the floor unconscious. Josh looked up to see the figure standing over Chris. She had a steel pipe in her hands.

Josh immediately stopped with a gasp. Then the Libyan stepped out from around the other corner with a handgun aimed directly at him. Josh stood frozen. At first, he was dazed with confusion, but he forced himself to voice his confounded question.

"Rachel? What are you doing?"

A helicopter landed about 300 yards from the ship. Max got out with three SWAT members. He pulled out his vest from his duffle bag and put it on. He holstered two Glocks on each leg, and he unzipped another large canvas bag and pulled out a UMP submachine gun. Then he headed for the Rusalka.

Three other FBI black SUVs were only minutes away.

Afon spoke up, "Were you actually trying to save these children?" He walked around Josh who was tied up in a chair. Afon continued, "And you attempted to do this alone? Just you and him?" He pointed to Chris who was still lying unconscious on the floor.

"Rachel, are you with him?" Josh asked. Rachel didn't say a word. Her blank, freakish stare was horrifying.

"She is," responds Afon. "With me, that is. Although somewhat against her inner will." Afon knelt down in front of Josh and smiled as he spoke. "You see, she is being controlled by my father's greatest invention. There is nothing she can do," he said as he glanced at her, "but obey what I say."

"What did you do to her?"

Afon stood up and walked behind Josh as he answered. "Rachel has been a part of my father's plan for quite some time now. About fifteen years, or so. She was injected with a microchip into her brain that receives electrical impulses from a supercomputer."

"What kind of supercomputer?" he asked.

Afon continued, "This supercomputer is located offsite, so don't try to figure out what you can do to save her. There is nothing you can do. Rachel is under my control."

Then Afon turned toward the Libyan. "Tie the other one up. Then wait here for my orders."

The Libyan woke Chris up as he was tying his wrists behind his back. Then he walked out of the room and closed the metal door.

Chris sat up against the wall. "Josh, I hope you have an idea," he moaned, "because I really wasn't planning on dying today."

"I'm thinking. I'm thinking," replied Josh. "OK. I think I've got it."

From a distance, a caravan of three Toyota minivans approached cautiously. As they came to a stop the leader exited his van and noticed the black SUVs parked inconspicuously. The middle-eastern man motioned for the others to get out of the vans. Then they loaded their Uzis and AK-47s and made their plan of attack.

The leader pulled out a pair of binoculars and looked closely at the ship. He noticed the FBI SWAT. Then he noticed someone else. Someone familiar.

He slowly brought the binoculars down. "Max McClain," said Amir Nasab with a smile.

The SWAT team advanced inside the ship. They threw smoke bombs in strategic places to avoid being seen. Their orders were to free the children and only to shoot the enemy if necessary.

Someone pounded on the inside of the metal door shouting, "Help! Help me!" The Libyan turned toward the door, raised his firearm, and put his hand on the door handle. The pounding and shouting stopped, and he heard a thud on the floor inside the room. He slowly opened the door and saw one of the captives lying face down on the floor. The other was missing.

He cautiously walked into the room with his weapon aimed at the body on the floor. Suddenly, Josh jumped down on top of him from the ceiling, grabbing the gun with his tied hands. Chris jumped up from the floor and started punching the Libyan in the face. The Libyan began shouting in Arabic, and then he pulled the trigger releasing several rounds inside the metal room.

Max led two SWAT teams through the corridors of the ship. Each man wore goggles to see through the smoke. Suddenly shots were fired, and Max stopped in his tracks. It was hard to determine the direction of the shots inside the metal ship.

They ran back the other way, hearing shouts in a foreign language. The shots stopped, and Max heard Josh yelling. "Chris! Chris!" Max found them inside a room. Josh was kneeling over Chris who was on the floor, leaned up against the wall. His hand was covering his left shoulder.

Max carefully grabbed Chris' hand and moved it away from his shoulder. It revealed a bullet hole and lots of blood.

"OK, Josh, you stay with Chris," Max said. He reached in a pocket and pulled out a blue bandana. "Press this hard against the wound. It will slow the bleeding. The shot went through—it missed major vessels, so you'll be OK."

"Max, I'm sorry," said Josh. "I know we shouldn't be here. But—"

"Let's not worry about that now," interjected Max. "We're gonna get these kids." Max looked over at the Libyan's body lying lifeless on the cold, metal floor. It occurred to him what Josh and Chris had to do. He turned to Josh. "Are you OK?" he asked. "Steady?"

Josh looked at the body and then back at Max. "Yeah, I'm good." Chris nodded, indicating that he was OK.

"Max," Josh continued, "Rachel's not. Something's happened to her—she's been brainwashed, or something. Afon is mind-controlling her somehow."

"Mind-controlling?" asked Max.

"Yeah. He said something about an off-site supercomputer that controls a microchip implanted in her head. Do you think it could be that room of electronics you saw at the farmhouse in Conroe?"

"Could very well be," Max replied.

"Max, she definitely was not herself. She actually knocked Chris out. And she was all zombie-like." Josh waved his arms in zombie-like fashion as he said that.

Max looked away. "He's finally done it."

Just then, Max and each SWAT team member put a hand over his left ear. Josh sat up straight, wondering what they were hearing in their ear pieces.

"We've been called to the main deck, Josh. You stay in here with Chris." With that, Max shut the door behind him.

As they made their way to the main deck, Max radioed FBI HQ, "We need to take out the farmhouse. Everything in it must be destroyed."

"Max, Nichols might want to check things out there," answered the agent from HQ.

"I don't have time to explain. You have to trust me."

They cautiously advanced to the main deck and hid behind a large container. From their angle they could see three middle-eastern men with AK-47s aimed at two SWAT team members. Max got low and crawled to get a better view.

"Oh no."

Chris moaned in pain.

"Seems like we were in this situation not too long ago," said Josh, recalling the event at Chris' house during the hurricane.

"Yeah. Seems we just have an attraction for danger, huh?"

"Seems that way," Josh said with a smile.

"Josh."

"Yeah?"

"I dunno if we're gonna make it out of this alive. So I want you to know that—" Chris took in a deep breath, trying to remain calm despite the pain in his shoulder. "—I regret missing the last three years of your life. You mean a lot to me, brother."

Josh closed his eyes for a second. He looked away. Then, turning back to Chris, he said, "Remember when Dad used to take us fishin' every other Saturday? Remember that day when you and I got into it really bad over a spinner bait? We both wanted the same one."

"We were, what? Twelve? Thirteen?" chuckled Chris.

Josh laughed. "Somethin' like that, yeah. Remember how mad Dad got?"

"Yeah, I do. Man, he did get mad."

"I remember what he said to us." Josh mimicked their dad's deep voice, "'Boys, one day you may live in different states and hardly ever see each other. Don't waste this time now.'"

The two laughed out loud, but then Chris groaned in pain. "Oh, don't make me laugh, Josh! Don't make me laugh!"

The two settled. "Wow. I do remember that," Chris said. "I think at that time we were hoping to live states apart. Man, I miss him."

"Yeah, so do I," said Josh. "You know, Chris. We have this time now. We're not wasting this time now." There wasn't much else said. Their expressions in the silence told the whole story. Josh held up his right hand, and Chris grabbed it and held on tightly.

"You mean a lot to me, too," said Josh.

"I don't wanna stay here, Josh." Chris began to get up.

"But Max told us to stay here."

"We die in here; we die out there. I'm not gonna die just sittin' around doing nothin'," said Chris, standing to his feet.

"But you've been shot!"

Chris looked at the Libyan's body on the floor. "I'll be fine. Grab his guns, and let's go to the deck."

CHAPTER TWELVE

"As-Salamu Alaykum."

Amir Nasab had a steady aim on Max's head on the ship's deck.
He had brought with him a small army of well-armed men. The SWAT had
their hands behind their heads and were all on their knees; each one had an
AK-47 pointed at his head by the surrounding Libyan mercenaries. Afon
stood next to Nasab, but Rachel was nowhere to be seen.

"It seems we have finally come to a conclusion, McClain," said
Nasab. "After fifteen years I've finally caught up with you. Your daring
escape from my prison was quite a feat, but you won't get away this time."

With his hands behind his head, Max slowly walked toward Nasab
who kept his steady aim on Max. Josh and Chris silently approached a
stack of barrels to hide behind and watch.

"That's right, Nasab. I escaped your maximum security. I overcame your armed guards, blew up your towers, and, in the process, your only son was killed before he could take another innocent life." Max's voice was stern and solid.

"What is he doing?" asked Chris.

"I don't know. He's gonna get himself killed," Josh replied.

Suddenly, Rachel showed up out of nowhere, and with her were the four kidnapped orphans. She had tied ropes around their necks and led them around like dogs. Max was astonished at the drastic change in her. She was so compassionate for the kids at the hospital, but now she treated them like animals.

"So what is it now, McClain? How are you going to save yourself now?" asked Nasab. "I have what I want."

"No, you don't. You don't have your scientist anymore. We've got him," replied Max.

Nasab's smile left his face. Keeping his pistol on Max, Nasab turned to Afon and whispered something. They conversed for a few seconds, and then Nasab turned his attention back to Max.

"Then it appears I will be needing you no longer. McClain, a life for a life. You took my son's life, now you will lose yours." Nasab steadied his aim at Max.

"Wait! Take me with you." shouted Max.

Nasab paused and squinted his eyes.

"Take me with you, Nasab! Trade me for the orphans. I'll go with you willingly; just let them go free with these men. Vladimir was wrong—they don't have the disease. They're no good for your experiments."

Nasab didn't move. His frame was solid. His pistol dead-aimed at Max's head. What took ten seconds seemed more like ten minutes.

"Come on, Nasab! You've wanted me for fifteen years!" shouted Max.

Nasab talked again with Afon. Max could barely hear their conversation, but he could tell Nasab was asking about the children and the disease he thought they had. Apparently, Afon confirmed Max's statement.

"That sounds appealing." Nasab lowered his aim. "Release the children," he ordered.

"Nasab! What about our orders?" yelled one of his men.

"Gaddafi is The Guide, but my family comes first!" Nasab said as he got into the face of his protestor. He gave Max a vicious stare.

Josh and Chris watched as Rachel released the children, and the SWAT carefully approached them and surrounded them. The children were finally safe, it seemed, but Josh and Chris had no idea what to expect next.

The calm of the sunny, blue sky in Conroe was abruptly interrupted by two F/A-18 Hornets screaming by at near supersonic speed. They quickly approached their target: the old farmhouse where Sokolov's supercomputer existed. A missile dropped beneath the forward jet and propelled itself ahead. The searing sound and thin line of smoke streaked across the sky, and the missile entered the center of the farmhouse.

Like a gigantic balloon expanding with fire and black smoke, the property exploded with crushed lumber and debris flying outward. The thundering, ear-popping booms could be heard for miles all around.

"Target destroyed. Returning to base." said the pilot as the Hornets screamed away.

Josh and Chris watched Max get on his knees. His hands were behind his head. Two Libyan men, armed with AKs, rushed to him and ordered him to lay flat on his stomach. One of them kicked him in the side, and Max yelled and moaned. Josh desperately wanted to jump out and try to save his friend, but he knew it would be suicide.

Max took another kick to the same side, followed by another to the head. It was a severe beating, and Josh and Chris sat there watching the whole thing. There was nothing they could do. With his brother losing blood fast and his best friend being beaten and taken captive by mercenaries, Josh's heart pounded with fear, anxiety, and anger all at once.

His eyes teared up. He rocked back and forth on his knees—wanting to do something but knowing he couldn't. He was so worn out—so tired of this battle. Now it was hopeless for Max.

The men tied Max's hands behind his back and 2 of them each grabbed an arm and dragged him down the ship's ramp. They shoved him into the back of Nasab's vehicle, and the rest of them got into their minivans.

As Nasab walked over to his van he dialed a number in his cell phone and put it to his ear. In Arabic, he ordered for the helicopter to meet them at the rendezvous. Then he got into his van, and the three vehicles drove away.

Rachel blinked her burning eyes; it felt like she hadn't closed them in hours. Her throat was dry and sore. Her eyes began to water, sending tears down her soft face. She felt like she was just rudely awakened from a long, deep sleep—sluggish and dragging. Every muscle in her body was tired and achy, and she began to weep as she fell to her knees.

Josh knew he would never see his friend again. His breathing was heavy, and his adrenaline was shooting through every vein his body. He saw Afon steal a unit from a port authority officer and drive off, so Josh jumped up and ran over to his truck. He started it up and sped off after Afon.

Then Chris stood to his feet. "What's your problem?" He shouted as he hobbled up to the nearest SWAT member. "You just let him go! You just let them take Max! You did nothing!"

"We didn't just let Max go. This is part of the plan."

"Max's plan, actually," chimed in one of the men whom Chris had seen with Max on the ship.

"Plan? What plan?" Chris asked, still holding the bandana to his shoulder.

Rachel, having come to her senses, rushed over to the children. They were hunkered down—huddled with one another—frightened and crying. She knelt down in front of them and tried to speak calmly.

"Hey, it's OK." She realized the kids were afraid of her, but she wanted to show that she had not been herself. She desperately wanted to prove that she really loved them.

Her heart was torn for how she realized she had treated them, albeit, against her will. "You poor kids have been through so much these last few days. All you wanted was someone to love you, and you got all this. I am so sorry," she said as she removed the ropes from their necks.

It was that last sentence Rachel said that brought out one of the children. The little girl took two small steps toward Rachel. Rachel repeated with a quivering voice, "I am so—so very sorry." Her tears sparkled in the sunlight as they trickled down her face.

The little girl replied with one English word, "OK?"

Rachel perked up, "What, honey?"

The little girl pointed to Rachel. "You OK?"

Rachel immediately grinned from ear to ear, but her grin quickly turned to weeping. "Yes! Oh, yes, sweetheart! I'm OK!" And she hugged the little one. The other children looked at each other in wonder. Then they followed their friend and embraced Rachel. Their forgiveness was overwhelming.

The minivans pulled into the parking lot of an abandoned warehouse where a helicopter had just landed. Max was in the middle bench seat of the van—eyes closed and holding his side. He knew he had suffered broken ribs and a split over his right eye. When the vans came to a stop, he opened his eyes.

Chris was led to another set of FBI units that had just arrived. "Why are we not using the ones you came in?" he asked.

"Those? Oh, they're set to explode on ignition. Those crazy Libyans," replied one of the SWAT. "Come on. We gotta get you to a hospital."

The van Max and Nasab were in was in between the other two. Before the men could get out of the vans, Max slowly raised his left hand toward his mouth. Nasab noticed and looked at him with a confused face. Max, staring calmly into Nasab's eyes, spoke into the underside of his wristwatch.

"Blow it."

Suddenly, the vans on both sides of Max exploded, sending shockwaves to both sides of Nasab's van. Max quickly pulled out a knife hidden inside his vest. He grabbed Nasab's head in front of him with his left hand and held the knife to his throat with his right.

"Tell your driver to place both hands on the steering wheel," Max said to Nasab, who quickly gave the orders in Arabic. Max reached into the driver's shoulder holster and grabbed his gun. Then he did the same with Nasab. "Now get out. Let's go! To the chopper!" shouted Max.

All three ducked as they ran to the door of the helicopter. With a gun aimed at both men, Max ordered Nasab in first. Then he got in, and as the driver was about to step in, Max thrust his right foot to the driver's forehead—causing him to fly backward to the ground. Max shut the door and demanded the pilot to take off.

Max kept his gun on Nasab while they both put on their headsets. "Alright, Amir. Take me to your sleeper cell."

"You can't get in there. There's only one of you, and we have at least two dozen men. What do you expect to do?"

"You let me worry about the details. Now order your pilot to take me to your crew."

The helicopter rose into the air and headed north.

Isabella opened her eyes. Her skull fracture was healing well, and she was breathing on her own. Because she was one of the Peruvian orphans, she had been transferred to the Texas Children's Hospital in Houston. Her best friend, Kristina, was able to travel with her.

"The doctors in Lake Charles felt it would be good for Isabella if Kristina came along," said the accompanying nurse to the doctor in charge.

"I understand. We'll take good care of her. You folks did a great job with her," replied the doctor. "Come on, Kristina. You must be hungry. How about some dinner?" The doctor took Kristina by the hand and thanked the nurse. The nurse thanked him back, and then returned to Lake Charles.

Kristina leaned over and kissed her friend on the forehead. "Hola, Isa. Como?" Isabella looked at her friend and a smile formed on her tired face.

"No, don't land!" said Max. "Hover at forty feet!"

Nasab just looked at Max. He couldn't believe what was happening.

"Tell him, Nasab!" shouted Max.

Nasab gave the orders to the pilot. After two minutes of hovering, his curiosity got the best of him. "What are we doing, McClain?"

Max didn't answer. He had that determined look on his face, and his pistol was well-sighted on Nasab. Nasab understood that he could never be quick enough to overtake Max. He wouldn't dare even to try.

Three more minutes went by, and then the men noticed several black SUVs surround the compound. Nasab looked at Max. His eyes were wide with confusion.

Max reached into his vest pocket and pulled out a square-shaped computer chip and held it up for Nasab to see.

"GPS! Ain't technology great?" Max said with a smile.

Nasab didn't say a word.

Josh had Afon's vehicle in sight. His heart was racing as fast as his truck was speeding down State Highway 225. Afon noticed Josh's truck weaving between traffic trying to catch up, so he floored it. Josh moved into the far left lane, but realized there were too many cars. He jerked onto the left shoulder and sped up, bypassing dozens of cars.

Afon's unit flew by an HPD officer who immediately turned on his lights and took off after him. The officer looked to his left and saw Josh's truck speeding down the shoulder, so he called in backup.

At the last split second, Afon took an exit ramp off to the right. The cop followed. Josh slammed on his brakes and maneuvered his truck through the traffic toward the upcoming exit. Cars were screeching to a halt, and one of them plowed into the back of another. But Josh continued.

"Suspect is heading North on Independence Parkway!" shouted the officer into his radio. A pedestrian started to walk across the parkway, not realizing the fast approaching caravan. Afon flew by, but the officer had to swerve to miss. He lost control of his vehicle and crashed into a telephone pole.

Josh was catching up. They were flying through a section of refineries, passed through red lights, causing cars to slam on their brakes and run into each other.

Finally, Josh was able to maneuver his truck alongside Afon. He swerved into Afon's lane, trying to push him off the road. Afon's unit treaded partially through a ditch, but gained control and sped back up. Then he tried to ram the side of Josh's truck.

Suddenly, Josh saw Afon pull out a gun. Afon shot Josh's passenger-side window, missing him by inches. Josh jerked his truck into Afon again, and the impact caused Afon to drop his gun.

Just then, Josh noticed something up ahead. It had a tall smoke stack and huge artillery guns. It was the Battleship Texas harbored near the parkway. He knew three quarters of mile past that battleship was the end of the road. Josh didn't want Afon to realize the approaching demise, so he kept his attention on him by ramming the side of his unit.

The ramming continued as they flew by the battleship. They raced onward and, at about 500 feet before the ending, Josh braked hard and swerved behind Afon. Then he punched the accelerator and rear ended Afon's unit, pushing him along. At first, Afon didn't know what Josh was up to, but as soon as he looked up ahead, he slammed on his brakes.

It was too late. His unit plowed through the barricade with Josh directly behind him. Both vehicles soared through the air and plunged nose first into the Houston Ship Channel.

Josh unbuckled his seatbelt and tried to open his door. Water was gushing through the bottom fast, and his door was jammed. He reached into his glove compartment and grabbed his hunting knife. With the handle end, he broke his driver's side window which released an incredible influx of water into his truck. He crawled out of his sinking truck and swam to the surface.

Out of breath, Josh made his way to the bank of the channel and rested on all fours. After about a minute he stood up and began searching for Afon. Suddenly, he heard someone running up behind him.

He turned and saw Afon leap toward him. Afon plowed into Josh, and both men went down on the beach. Josh jumped to his feet. Then, something seemingly overcame him—a strength he had not felt before.

It was a sudden and massive MMA match that happened with incredible speed. Josh did not wait for his opponent to swing first; he stepped in close, throwing Afon off guard, and swung a right hook into his jaw, followed by a quick thrust with his left fist to the rib cage. Afon yelled in pain, but mustered enough energy to take a jab back at Josh. Josh grabbed the jab and threw Afon to the ground.

Workers from the battleship had seen the two vehicles plunge into the channel and rushed to the scene. One of them saw Josh and Afon and yelled for everyone to watch. Quickly, about thirty people gathered to see the contest between the two men.

"You've lost, Afon," Josh said. "We have the children, we have your father, and now I've got you." Afon stared at him from the ground.

Then, with sudden force, Afon threw his right leg up and kicked Josh in the back of the head. He jumped to his feet and charged Josh with another punch. Josh deflected his punch, threw another jab to the ribs, and then slammed an uppercut.

Then Josh felt an incredible power rise from deep within. He jumped up with a massive front kick straight to Afon's chest. The powerful thrust caused Afon to fly backward onto his back. The match was over.

HPD and FBI units rushed to the scene. They saw Josh standing alone on the beach. He saw the officers approach him and then looked down to see his defeated opponent. Then he noticed Max get out of the car and walk toward him. The officers handcuffed Afon, but they had to carry their unconscious enemy to their units.

"How are you?" asked Max.

"Right now?" Josh said. "I'm doing pretty good." Josh noticed a few cuts and bruises on Max's face. "Looks like I'm doing a little better than you," he said jokingly.

Max smiled and put his arm around Josh as the two walked toward the units. Then he said, "So do you think it might be a good time to clear your head again?"

Josh smiled. "I'm ready to go home."

The next morning, Josh walked into Chris' hospital room. Chris was sitting up eating his breakfast.

"Man, you recover fast, bro," said Josh.

"I've had practice. By the way, thanks for the blood."

Josh gave his brother a smile. Then Chris' attention was directed to the doorway. Josh turned around and saw Rachel standing with a worried countenance—surely she was embarrassed at what she had done. It was quiet at first, but Josh broke the awkwardness of the moment, "Hey, how are you?"

Rachel sighed deeply. "Hi. Can I come in?"

"Yeah, of course," said Josh.

"How are you feeling?" asked Chris.

"Oh, I'm—fine. How are you?"

"I think I'll make it," said Chris.

"Chris, I am—so—sorry." Rachel lower lip quivered as she spoke.

"Ah, it's OK, Rachel." Again, it got quiet. "So remind me to never get on your bad side, alright?" he said with a smile.

Josh laughed, and Rachel smiled.

"There it is," said Josh. "There's that smile. How are you really doing?" he asked as he walked toward her.

Rachel looked down, but Josh gently lifted her face to look at him. "Rachel, it's OK. We understand. It's not your fault."

She fell apart in tears, and Josh pulled her into his embrace. "It's OK. It's all over, Rachel. It's all over," he said as he held her gently.

"Alright," interjected Chris with a mouth full of food. "Come on! I'm trying to eat my breakfast, here."

Josh and Rachel laughed. Rachel sat down in the chair, and Josh sat next to her.

"So what did the doctors say?" Josh asked Rachel.

Rachel wiped her tears with her sleeve as she answered, "Well, since the supercomputer is destroyed they're not too worried, but they are scheduling to remove the chip in a couple days."

"That's good. That's very good," Josh replied.

"Oh, and I called Naomi. She's doing great. We're reorganizing the foster homes for the children. They had been staying at Camp Pinerock, but when we opened up the opportunity for foster care, we were flooded with calls."

"Caroline Springs is a changed town," said Josh, smiling at Chris.

"Yes, and—well, those families are already talking of permanent adoption," replied Rachel.

"Wait. You mean—all the kids have been placed?" Chris asked.

"Yes! All of them! In less than a day. We've never seen anything like this."

Josh looked at Chris. They both knew what each other was thinking. Max and Stella had been anxious about adopting one of these children.

"So there's the man of the hour," said Special Agent-in-charge Brian Nichols as he walked into Max's hospital room. A nurse was tightly wrapping Max's mid-section to keep his ribs immobile. Sitting on the side of the bed, Max looked up and smiled at Nichols, who extended his hand. Max shook it.

"You did good, Max. You did very good."

"Thanks Brian. That means a lot coming from you," Max said with a big smile.

"Listen. I'll cut to the chase, here. I had a good talk with the Director, and, uh—"

"No," Max interrupted. "No, Brian. I don't want to be reinstated."

Brian paused, tilted his head, and then smiled. "You sure?" he asked. "Full benefits. I hear you don't get much of that at that camp of yours."

Max smiled as he replied, "I'm sure. Thanks."

"OK," said Nichols with an inflection in his voice that expressed honor. He began to walk out of the room but stopped and turned back around toward Max. "It's those kids," he said smiling. "Isn't it? Those darn kids have you wrapped around their fingers," he said jokingly.

Max smiled and placed his hand over his heart. "You got me."

Nichols smiled back, slapped the door frame, and left the room. Stella walked in from the opposite direction. She had noticed Nichols leaving Max's room. "What did he have to say?"

"Oh, you know—just checkin' in on me."

"Right. He offered you a position, didn't he?"

Max smiled at his bride. Stella had always been the only one to whom he was unable to lie. Then Rachel knocked on the door frame. As soon as Stella saw her, she walked over and hugged her.

"How are you, sweetie?" said Stella.

"I'm OK. Got a little headache, but I'll be fine."

"Have a seat, Rachel," said Max.

"Well, actually, I need to talk to you, two, about something." Rachel had a serious look on her face. Max and Stella looked at each other in wonder and then looked back at Rachel.

"OK. What is it? Sounds serious," said Stella.

Rachel breathed in deeply and sighed. "It's about the orphans."

Stella gave a forced smile. "Oh, honey, we already know. Josh was in here earlier and told us. We're very glad they are all placed. That's very good news."

Rachel's serious look turned into a gentle smile. "Well, then you haven't heard all the news."

CHAPTER THIRTEEN

The nurse was reading aloud a children's story in Spanish to Kristina and Isabella in the hospital room at Texas Children's. Rachel stood at the door for a few seconds and smiled as she watched. Then the nurse noticed her and put the book down. She told the girls that she would finish it later.

"Hi, I'm Rachel."

"Hi, Rachel. My name is Summer. I'm taking the day shift today."

"Oh, good. You are doing really well with them," Rachel said, looking at the girls. "It's great that you can speak their language. Makes them feel at home. So, how is she doing?"

"Oh, she's doing well. She's still not speaking, but her injuries are healing well."

"Summer, I have a couple of friends here who would like to spend some time with Isabella. Would it be OK if they came in now?" asked Rachel.

"Sure. I'll just be at the nurses' station. Call me if you need me."

Max and Stella walked in cautiously behind Rachel, as if they were trying not to wake up someone. Max's heartbeat was fast. He thought it was amazing that he could go through the previous day's events without a second's thought, but this event chilled his nerves.

Stella, holding his hand, felt a knot forming in her stomach. She only felt that way when she was about to speak in public or fly in a plane, but this knot was different—a tremendous anticipation that could lead to extravagant joy or deep disappointment. She looked at her husband and gave a look that spoke a thousand endearing words all at once.

Rachel led them to the bedside. "This is Kristina—Isabella's best friend. She's been by her side this whole time. She's pretty much Isabella's voice these days." Kristina greeted the visitors in her language.

"And this is Isabella. We call her Isa for short." Rachel turned to Isabella and, in Spanish, told her who Max and Stella were. She explained that Max and Stella wanted to know if she would like to stay with them when she leaves the hospital. As Rachel talked, Max and Stella stared at the beautiful little girl.

Tremendous thoughts ran through their heads. Dreams of a family, road trips, Christmas and other holidays—all things a family would do. Deep-seeded, earnest prayers welled up from within their hearts to the Lord for the long awaited dream to come true.

Stella leaned in close and, in Spanish, she said, "Hello, Isabella. Hello, Kristina. It is so good to meet you. My name is Stella, and this is

Max—my husband." She paused. She didn't know what to say next, and a lump formed in her throat.

Rachel took over. "Would you like to go stay with them? Would you like to go to their home?" Kristina looked at her friend lying in the bed. With bandages wrapped around her head, Isabella had a very serious face. The adults in the room recognized that they would have to settle for facial expressions from Isabella.

Rachel continued, "You can stay there for a little while. It will be just like we started. You could stay with them and have a chance to meet some great people—many people who are wanting to adopt."

The room got quiet. Rachel turned to look at Max and Stella. Suddenly, they heard a little voice.

"Casa?"

Rachel quickly looked toward the hospital bed. It was Isabella.

"What? Did you just say something, honey?" asked Rachel with a straight face.

"Hogar?" Isabella responded. Then she said it in English. "Home?"

Stella covered her mouth with both hands and gasped. Max leaned in a little closer to Isabella. "Yes, honey. Home."

Rachel's eyes filled with tears. Max stepped back and cleared his throat. Stella closed her eyes. Tears streamed down her face and her heart leaped. "Oh, Lord, please," she prayed.

Then Isabella looked at Kristina who was smiling at her friend. It was clear she was happy for Isa, but Isa grabbed her friend's hand and squeezed. She looked up at Rachel and said, "Kristina?"

Rachel quickly spoke up, "Oh, Isa. And Kristina!"

"Yes!" said Stella. "Oh, honey, we want to take both of you!"

For the first time in several months, Isa spoke. And her words brought an incredible wealth of emotions to the adults. They embraced and cried together—tears of near-unbelievable joy.

"You know what?" Rachel asked the McClains. "The thought occurred to me. If Isabella had not been hurt, you would have not had the chance to adopt her and Kristina. They would have been at the camp and fostered out with the others. But they came here." Rachel turned to look at the girls. "God prepared them for you. He used something painful to bring something so precious to you—and to them."

"And instead of one little girl," Stella said, "He gave us two."

Two hours later Max was in his room about to be discharged. Josh and Chris were celebrating the good news of Max and Stella's newest additions to their families.

Max's doctor walked in with his chart in hand. "Well, Mr. McClain, all I need you to do is sign a couple forms, and then you're good to go," said the doctor.

"Good," replied Stella. "We have a lot of work to do at Pinerock. CEF has moved in and is making great headway. The Radius Initiative is already a go!"

"You know, it's really amazing," Chris said. "We were risking our lives to reach these children. And back at Pinerock, here comes a group who wants to do the same."

"It is amazing," interrupted Rachel as she walked in the room. "And I was heading in the opposite direction when y'all reached out to me. You didn't have to do that—you saved my life." Rachel looked down. "There's nothing I want to do more than to reach out to children."

The doctor listened to their conversation. It wasn't every day that he met a group of people who nearly lost their lives in order to save the lives of someone else. And to hear the parallels between their ordeal and the work with this group called CEF brought interest to him.

"So this group you mentioned, CEF—they reach out to children? Where are they located?" asked the doctor.

"Most everywhere. They're in about 170 countries," replied Stella. "Now they're partnering with us and several area churches in Louisiana to reach kids with the gospel, help nurture them and their families, and get them plugged into churches."

"You know what?" replied the doctor as he removed his eye glasses. "A group of friends and I were just talking about starting a nonprofit to work with kids. We are prepared to put up a good bit of money to get it going. But this sounds a lot like what we're trying to do. Perhaps we could just support CEF, instead."

"Well, I'm sure they would accept your assistance," responded Max.

"Well, I'll just have to look into that," said the doctor. "By the way, Mr. McClain, you sure took a beating."

"Yeah," laughed Josh. "You should've seen it! We're all glad he's got a hard head."

"Well, I'm glad," the doctor paused, "that you're doing very well. I'm sure you're feeling—just fine." The doctor greeted everyone and left the room, but he mistakenly left Max's medical chart on the counter near Chris.

"Feeling fine?" argued Rachel. "Max, you look horrible!"

"Gee, thanks," Max said laughing.

Chris gingerly glanced at Max's record and noticed something strange. He leaned in closer to get a better look when he noticed the words CONGENITAL SENSITIVITY TO PAIN. In a snap he looked up at Max.

"What?" Max shrugged his shoulders.

"Is there anything else about you we don't know?"

"Maybe," Max replied smiling. "But it's all classified."

Two Months Later—Mitu, Columbia, South America

A small group of missionaries from America were praying over twelve Columbian orphans in a remote village not far from Mitu, Columbia. The orphans were about to be sent to a few families in the U. S. One of the missionaries leaned over to ask a question to his translator.

"Who is she?"

"I do not know. I have never seen her before, but her prayer for the children was very interesting," answered the translator.

"Why? What did she say?"

"She asked God to give to these children special ability, or powers."

"Powers? What kind of powers?"

The translator turned to the missionary with a half embarrassed look. "Well—to knock down walls. What could this mean?"

The missionary squinted his eyes in wonder and thought. "She looks quite old. Perhaps she's not thinking clearly," replied the missionary.

The elderly lady stopped at the doorway, turned around to face the missionary, and she smiled.

ABOUT THE AUTHOR

J. Chad Barrett is the Director of Child Evangelism Fellowship of Houston, Texas. Along with his writing career, Chad is an engaging speaker and musician. His personal ministry, Inspiring Evangelism, enables him to inspire and train Christians to share the good news of Jesus Christ.

Chad lives in Houston, Texas with his wife and four children. And a dog and cat.

Visit his blog at www.InspiringEvangelism.com.

www.ingramcontent.com/pod-product-compliance
Lightning Source LLC
Chambersburg PA
CBHW071251130626

46556CB00003B/1263